THE MULE THIEVES

ALSO BY JAMES POWELL

A Summer with Outlaws
Apache Moon
The Hunt
The Malpais Rider
A Man Made for Trouble
Deathwind
Stage to Seven Springs
Vendetta

THE MULE THIEVES

PROLOGUE

A man who encounters snow at nine thousand feet shouldn't be surprised. Not even in early April, he shouldn't.

Pete Ware knew that when he set out. He wore a heavy sheepskin coat, rode a good horse, and he had provisions enough in his bedroll for several days stay, if need be. It was something he had to do, a place he had to go. He had never intended to go back, but now it wasn't a matter of choice.

He wasn't a young man; he remembered the day he'd turned fifty with stark clarity.

He had not come alone, but somewhere back there he had lost his only companion. Rutherford's boy, the damn fool. Ware had not wanted him along in the first place, but now it was even more imperative than before that he do what he had come to do and get back out.

Trouble was, this was only his second time in these mountains, and he had come in from the north when his route the other time had been from the south. Maybe that explained why he had spent one day half-lost already. Too many things just didn't look the same.

He had hoped for better weather. He didn't need any bad luck. But here he was, snowflakes as large as his thumb floating down so thick he almost couldn't see his horse's ears. A gray dawn from the beginning, the weather had grown only worse as time went along.

Well behind him now was a high peak called Withington; somewhere to the south were more high peaks. He could not see them, if not for the snow and clouds, then for the tall pine that surrounded him. Somewhere near, however, was the canyon, its sides steep and rocky and heavily timbered, his destination. There was a tiny cave down there, near a spring with clear water, both hard to find. He had hidden something there once, many years ago; something he was not proud of then and was ashamed of even now. But the time had come when he must go back for it.

It wasn't personal gain he was concerned with. He had turned away from that years ago, buried all thoughts of it with his guilt in that cave. But he wasn't the only one involved. Time and someone else had caught up with him. He was forced to come back.

He had told them to give him a month; a month and he would return. There were good reasons why he must honor his word.

He had done what he'd done then for a young wife and two little girls. He did what he was doing now for the memory of the one and the future of the other two.

He had come to the mountains careful not to be seen by other than his lone companion. They had stopped to ask a thing of no one. They had purchased provisions at a place fifty miles away and had traveled from that place under cover of the night. Now Ware was alone again.

He just wished the weather had held. He wished he knew better how close he was to the right canyon, the spring, and the cave. He had been thinking he might be very close indeed.

The ground ahead of him was wet and slick, the slope he was on high and exposed. He had no choice but to go on, at least till he found a decent place to camp. Maybe tomorrow he would have better luck. Right now he just wished his horse had a little better footing for the descent. . . .

CHAPTER 1

I was riding along leading these three mules and trying to remember exactly what I'd done the night before to make me feel so all over rotten when I noticed the girl. The sorrel cow pony I was riding must have noticed her at about the same time, for he stopped with a jerk and threw up his head and ears. The three mules behind me bumped into one another while following suit.

The girl simply sat there at the base of what was probably a two-century-old piñon that grew alongside the road, her back against the trunk of the tree and her arms resting loosely on her updrawn knees. She couldn't have been more than thirty yards away, yet for the longest moment she gave absolutely no notice of my little caravan. She just seemed to be staring straight ahead, toward her horse, which grazed with saddle on but bridle bit removed some ten or fifteen yards from where she sat.

But for her long brown hair, one might have thought her a boy. She was clad in the trousers, shirt, and vest of a cowhand, and beside her on the ground was a wide-brimmed felt hat. A bright spring sun beamed down through the branches of the tree. The streaks in her hair were more golden than brown.

She was no ordinary sight for such a place, yet I thought I had seen her somewhere before. If I hadn't had so much to drink the night before, I was sure I could remember when and where.

She finally turned her gaze my way as I spurred the sorrel toward her. It bothered me considerably that I could not recall where I had seen such a pretty face.

"Problems?" I asked as I drew up close to where she sat. The sun was hot on my back and my head felt about two sizes too large for my hat. I really didn't feel well at all.

She slowly got to her feet and swiped at the dust on her pants with her hat. She didn't seem at all surprised to have seen me come riding up.

"My horse is lame," she said simply.

I draped the lead rope of the nearest mule loosely over my saddle horn and dismounted. My horse would stand ground-reined well enough. The second and third mules were tied to the preceding mule's tail and stood docilely behind the leader.

I walked over to the girl's horse. The animal was a pretty gray gelding. "Lose a shoe or something?" I asked.

She shrugged. "I don't think so. He just pulled up lame. I don't know what it is."

I stared at her a moment. "Have we seen each other somewhere before? I mean, you look familiar . . ." I felt very foolish saying that.

She cocked her head guardedly. "I don't know. Have we?"

"My name is Kel O'Day," I told her. "Kel is for Kelly."

"That's nice. A nice name, either way," was all she said.

I shrugged and turned to the horse. "Which foot is it?"

She hesitated. "Which foot?" I repeated. "Where's he lame?"

"Oh . . . yes. Well, I'm not sure. I think the left front. Yes, that's the one."

I looked at her quizzically. She wasn't sure which foot the animal favored?

She didn't offer to say anything else, so I turned back to the horse. The animal had ceased grazing and was looking at me suspiciously. I reached out and ran my hand down its neck to its left shoulder and was about to progress this way on down its leg when a noise from behind me caused me to start.

I whirled around and saw that a man had suddenly appeared just a few yards to the girl's left, rifle in hand. He was a big, dark-complexioned fellow of about fifty, with a black, bushy beard and a slouch hat pulled low over his eyes. Before my surprise wore off from the sight of this first fellow, a second, seemingly younger man stepped from behind one of the many trees nearby. He, too, was dark and bearded and armed with a rifle. As was the case with the girl, I thought I'd seen both of these fellows before.

I noticed the girl sort of flinch and turn her head away, and I was in the midst of wondering about that when suddenly I heard a noise behind me again. I tried to turn but was too slow, and the next thing I knew something struck me hard and all went black after that.

Waking up was no joy. My head throbbed terribly. My face was against the ground and dirt was in my mouth. I gagged and threw up, then somehow managed to roll over. I couldn't stop heaving for several minutes. Just then, I would have given all I had for death just to go ahead and come.

For some time I lay on my back, trying to open my eyes. When I finally managed that task, the world was like a bright ball of fire, and I realized I was looking into a blinding midday sun.

Somehow I managed to get myself into a sitting position. Then I managed—by looking at the ground and not at the sky—to crack one eyelid. Then the other. Very slowly I raised my head. My neck felt as if someone had driven a spike into it; I could not straighten it.

I began trying to recall what had happened to me. My brain was as fuzzy as my eyesight. I had to think a minute before I could recall my own name.

All I seemed able to do was just sit there, looking around, my eyes still adjusting. Trees . . . I saw a lot of trees, mostly piñon, some juniper, but not so thick I couldn't see through and beyond them. Mountains lay in the distance, beyond a grassy plain, all very familiar. . . .

I felt the back of my head, and my hand came away bloody. What on earth had happened to me? Where was I?

I forced myself to look back toward the mountains. Finally it came to me. I not only knew those mountains, I knew them well. They were the San Mateos; this was Socorro County, New Mexico Territory. I was looking almost due south. Around to the right, along the western base of the mountains and less than fifteen miles away, was where I lived, my own section of duly filed-on ground, with a cabin on it I had built myself and base territory for my own small but growing herd of cows.

I was Kel O'Day, twenty-six years old, a Kansas farm boy turned cowhand, with ambitions to develop a full-fledged outfit of my own. I'd been seven years knocking around parts of western New Mexico and eastern Arizona territories; seven years riding for large outfits and small, learning things I never would have learned while trudging along behind one of my pa's well-worn plows back home.

But none of this did much to explain my current state of affairs. What had I been doing to wind up on the ground in such a way with blood on the back of my head?

And then I remembered the mules. Ah, yes, the mules....

For several years I'd known this fellow over on the Blue River of Arizona, a man who preferred mules over horses to ride. He had a fair-size outfit in rough country, and he wasn't a young man anymore—he was at least sixty, with not an easy year in the lot. And his reason for preferring mules was simple: Few mules are as wide across the back and withers as a horse; a stiff old man can straddle one with less spread on the pelvis and thus with a good deal less discomfort over the course of a long day's ride—or so my friend had long claimed.

Trouble is, good saddle mules aren't always easy to find. And I knew that old man was both in the market and would pay well for three or four good ones. So, two days back when

I had come across a fellow down near Socorro who was in a bind for some cash and had three good young mules broke to ride and for sale for a bargain, I just naturally thought how I might do my friend on the Blue River a favor and make a small profit for myself as well.

I had just sold some three-year-old steers for fourteen dollars a head a few days before and had just enough money to close the deal for the mules.

It was mid–May, and the days were growing long, so I'd made the twenty-six miles to the fast-growing railhead cow town of Magdalena along about dark. I had a friend there who could pasture the mules and my horse overnight, and I'd made the mistake of deciding to put in a little time at one of the local drinking establishments. As it turned out, I must have made every "water hole" in town, and the "little time" turned into all night. It was the first time in a while that I'd done anything like that, and I suppose you'd have to say I really made the most of it. I must have, for although I may never remember all or even much of what I did during the night, I sure do remember how I felt when I woke up in my friend's barn the next morning!

Still, I was determined to continue my trip over to the Blue River. Despite a throbbing head, I had made my start shortly past breakfast. Everything just kept on going downhill from there.

Well, that much of it came back pretty clearly as I sat there on the ground ... right up to the point when I had ridden up on the girl about fifteen miles out from Magdalena, with parts of the broad, open plains of San Agustin stretching both ahead of me and to my left and the triple peaks of the Tres Montosas rising above the trees on my right. Right up to the girl and her supposedly lame horse ... the big dark man with the bushy beard ... a second fellow who looked almost like the first, only younger ... and then my head exploding as someone hit me from behind....

I looked around, thinking once again about the mules.

They were nowhere to be seen. Neither was my horse. All were gone.

Was that what my attackers had wanted? The mules and my horse? Had they very carefully waylaid me—even left me for dead—for that? All I had left were the clothes I wore and my hat, which I now discovered lying a few feet away in the dust, its crown crumpled in the back.

I didn't even have a weapon. I owned a Winchester saddle gun, but it was just where I always carried it—on my saddle, with my horse. I also owned a handgun, a .44 caliber Colt revolver. Rarely did I ever take it out of my right saddlebag, which of course was also with my saddle and my horse.

Another thing I didn't have was water. I had a commanding thirst, but nary a drop to drink, or to wash the wound on my head with or to cool me off.

Again I looked around. I was on the main road between Magdalena and the tiny community of Datil, which was located at the base of a small mountain range that lay about twenty miles farther west. The area was used frequently as a driveway for cattle and sheep being brought to the railroad (a spur of the Santa Fe) at Magdalena. Someone might eventually come along and find me. I could simply wait until that happened, but as I looked up and down the road, I certainly wasn't encouraged. Not a soul could be seen in either direction.

Just thinking about my predicament began to make me mad. I had good money tied up in those mules, and I could ill afford to lose a good saddle horse, not to mention the saddle, rifle, and six-gun that had gone with the animal.

I decided I should at least get to my feet to see if I could so much as stand. I was some dizzy, and my head sure hadn't quit throbbing, but I finally made it upright. Presently I was able to take the few steps necessary to reach my hat and even managed to bend down to retrieve the thing. Then I started looking around for tracks. It didn't take me long to discover eight or nine sets taking off to the south, toward the San Mateos.

I considered this. Less than five miles away in that direction was a cow camp for the nearest ranch I knew about—technically a neighbor of mine—located near the base of the mountains. I couldn't see it because of the trees around me, but I knew where it was. The cow outfit was Eastern-owned, but I knew the fellow who was its foreman and several of its riders. It wouldn't be at all unusual for someone to be staying at the camp this time of year.

Also, between me and the cow camp was a windmill. I had drunk at the well there before and the water was not bad. Both the well and the cow camp were a lot closer than Magdalena, and I figured if I could just keep a steady pace, I could make the camp in something less than three hours.

Maybe my thinking wasn't much steadier than my legs just then, but moments later I started trudging slowly south.

CHAPTER 2

I had only to go a short distance before leaving the trees completely. Ahead and to my right were open grama grass plains, across which a man's view went all but unbroken. Only a mile or two to my left were hills; farther east rose the Magdalena range; on the skyline to the south were the San Mateo Mountains; more mountains yet ranged around to the west. I was still a bit dizzy, but my eyesight had returned to about normal and I could see clearly the tower and wheel of the windmill standing dead ahead, no more than a mile away. The cow camp was a dark patch on the landscape some three or four miles farther on.

The surface of the plains seemed to drop away in the foreground, then rise again in the distance. Although seemingly flat otherwise, the terrain between me and the cow camp was broken by a number of deep swales large enough to hide a number of men on horseback. Once I was sure I saw a tiny group of moving figures appear, coming from within one of these swales, top out on a low ridge, then go out of sight again on the other side of the ridge. At the time, they were probably within a mile of the cow camp. I could see scattered bunches of cattle here and there also, but none of these were moving along in the manner of that little band of figures.

I didn't know yet what good it was going to do me to know all this, for I sure couldn't walk fast enough to catch up to them. I was doing good just to stay on my feet. Probably only my thirst and the sight of that windmill kept me walking. I even got to feeling a little less light-headed as I went.

* * *

What seemed like half a day for me to finally reach the windmill probably amounted to no more than an hour. Seldom was there a spring day in New Mexico when not the slightest breeze stirred the air, but today was one of those exceptions. I just stood there in the shadow of the wooden tower and looked forlornly up at the big wheel with its fanlike blades and tail standing perfectly still and pumping nary a drop. Well, worse could always come to worst. A dozen or so feet away, at the end of a horizontal pipe that was connected to the vertical pipe that went into the well, was a trough hewn from a massive log, full of water. When the mill pumped, the trough filled, then overflowed into a large scooped-out earthen tank, brimming with moss and little wriggly critters and bugs that skipped across the water's surface. Too, the water in the earthen tank reeked with the smell of cow manure and urine. I chose the wooden trough, going down on my knees and scooping handfuls of water up to my mouth, then dousing my head in the water.

I was just getting to my feet, dripping, when I heard a noise behind me. I guess my day thus far was enough to make me a bit apprehensive about things going on at my back, because I turned so fast I suffered a momentary return of dizziness and almost lost my balance. The noise I'd heard was that of a horse clearing its nostrils.

How they got that close to me in open country without me seeing them sooner I had no idea, but there sat two riders not thirty yards away, one of them leading a saddled though riderless horse. I suppose I simply had not been paying much attention to my surroundings as I walked that last quarter of a mile or so to the windmill; or maybe they had been riding within a low swale back there a ways and I couldn't have seen them at a distance no matter how alert I was.

I guess the main thing is, I *knew* both men. What's more, that horse they were leading looked amazingly just like my sorrel cow pony—*was* my sorrel cow pony, in fact!

I just stood there gawking like an idiot as they pulled up in front of me. One of them was tall and slender and sat very upright in his saddle. The other was short and stocky and seemed to slump. Both had disbelieving looks on their faces.

"Hello, Monte, Ike," I finally said. Monte Preston was the stocky one, Ike Sanders the tall one. I knew them both pretty well and considered them a good pair of fellows. They worked for the cow outfit that owned the well and the camp across the way. "Where'd you come across my horse?"

Ike looked over at his companion. "I told you that Slant K brand was Kel's. Didn't I tell you so? That's it right there on the horse's left shoulder—Slant K, big as hell."

Monte shrugged. "Yeah, yeah. You told me. We found him a couple of miles to the west of here, Kel. Looked like he'd done some runnin'. One rein was broke short—probably from his steppin' on it—and his saddle was loose and hangin' to one side. What happened, anyway? He throw you off somewhere back there?"

I walked over to the horse and started to check things out. I couldn't see anything missing, including my lariat, which was coiled and hooked to the saddle horn by means of a split-looped leather saddle string and probably would have been the first thing to fall off had the saddle slipped to the wrong side. Somehow even my rifle was still in its boot.

"He didn't throw me, Monte," I said. "Most likely the worst thing he did was he didn't stand ground-tired when he was supposed to—and I suppose even that wasn't so bad. My guess is, if he'd done anything else he'd have got himself stolen right along with my mules."

"Stolen?" one cowboy echoed the other. Both men dismounted as Monte added, "Mules, Kel? What mules . . . ?"

I told them everything from the time I bought the mules in Socorro to my ill-advised celebration in Magdalena and my eventual encounter with the girl and whoever her companions were who had robbed me. I even showed them the back of my head where I'd been clubbed.

"And you only saw the two men and the girl?" Monte asked. "You never even saw who hit you?"

"If I had, do you think I would have stood there like a dummy and let him do it?" I retorted.

"Well, no," he said archly. "Course you wouldn't let him just sneak up behind you either. You were much too alert for that."

I just shook my head and didn't say anything. He was right, of course.

"You're probably lucky they didn't kill you," Ike pointed out. "You ever think of that?"

"Yeah, I thought of it. I figure that may be exactly what they thought they did."

Monte squinted at me. "And all they took were your mules?"

I nodded. "I thought sure they'd taken the horse, too. I guess he must have gotten away during the ruckus. The mules were probably easier to catch, or maybe they were all those fellows wanted in the first place, who knows...."

"Did you see which way they went? Their tracks, at least?"

Again I nodded. "I've been following them right along as I walked. I figure they watered their stock here at the mill and went on south. Once I even thought I saw them in the distance, headed in the direction of your outfit's cow camp over there. They probably have a good two hours on me by now, maybe more."

Monte considered this. "What were you gonna do about it? Chase 'em down on foot?"

I gave him what I hoped was a supremely patient look. "I was hoping to find someone at the camp who could at least loan me a horse and some gear. Till you showed up with my horse, wasn't much I *could* do but walk."

Monte smiled. "Yeah, well, you would've been in some luck anyway, even if we hadn't shown up. Our outfit's gettin' ready for a big gather and brandin' on this side of the plains. Probably be fifteen or twenty men come ridin' into that camp this afternoon or late tonight, mostly in small groups or pairs like Ike and me, and someone among 'em will be drivin' a remuda of horses. Yesterday or the day before, though, there wouldn't have been a soul there. Anytime in the last two weeks, as a matter of fact."

"My lucky day, all right," I said. "No doubt about that."

Monte straightened and fingered his bridle reins. "Well, we're goin' that way; you might as well ride along with us. You may not catch up to your mule thieves, but at least you'll get someplace where you can get some rest and something to eat. The way you look just now, I'd say you need both."

I couldn't argue with him about that. I didn't know how bad I looked, but I felt like something that had just been stepped on. Food and rest sure were commodities I'd enjoyed precious little of during the past twenty-four hours. I turned to tighten the cinch on my saddle and make sure the broken bridle rein was still long enough to use before mounting.

As I swung aboard the sorrel, Ike rode up alongside of me. "You know, Kel, I never did cotton much to mules myself. Sure would hate to be known as someone who'd steal one. Wouldn't you?"

"I suppose I could agree with that."

Ike said, "You look pretty peaked, Kel. Sure you're okay?"

"I'm fine," I lied, hoping desperately I wasn't going to fall off before we even got going.

Somehow I hung on, and as we rode, Monte said thoughtfully, "About those mule thieves, Kel; you say the girl was a pretty one? And you say you think you've seen 'em before somewhere? You still don't remember where . . . or when?"

I shook my head. "I keep thinking about it, but I just can't come up with anything. Maybe when my head clears I will. I just don't know."

Actually, I didn't even know if it would make any difference if I did remember. All I did know was they had my mules, and they had got them by busting me over the head and leaving me lying flat on my face, maybe for dead. I was bothered some by not being able to remember where I'd seen them before, but I was bothered much more by the thought that I might never see them again—them *or* my mules.

For some it might not have meant all that much—neither the mules nor the money I had spent on them. For me it meant a lot. Those steers I'd sold hadn't taken me just a day or two to raise. And what the mules cost me couldn't be earned in a whole summer of riding for a cow outfit, not to mention what I'd planned to clear on the deal when I sold them.

As we rode, I all but forgot about being dizzy, about the pain in my head and the dull ache in my belly. Without even trying, we were soon following the tracks of the mule thieves again, and they were heading as true as steel in the direction of the cow camp.

We had only begun to think this curious when we became aware of something stranger yet. It was hard to be certain, for the sounds were very distant and not altogether distinct, yet we sure thought we heard the faint reports of rifles being fired from up ahead.

CHAPTER 3

THE shooting seemed to die off not long after it had started, except that every now and then a dull report could be heard that both Monte and Ike insisted probably came from a .44-40 Winchester rifle. And the closer we came to the cow camp the more convinced we became that the shots had come all along from there.

It took us less than an hour of steady riding to get there, yet midafternoon had come and gone and the sun was well to our right by the time we reached a point within about three hundred yards of the place. Because any further approach had to continue across open ground, we pulled to a halt, thinking to size things up first.

The layout of the camp was a pretty routine one. Most of it I knew about already because I had seen the place at least a dozen times before. Set between a pair of modest-size cottonwoods was a bunkhouse with cookshack built of pine logs hauled down from the San Mateos. Across from the house was a low-roofed barn and a sizable set of corrals. Behind the house was a cistern that was filled by spring water piped from about a mile away and a cellar that even at much closer quarters might go unnoticed except for a mound of earth with a stovepipe sticking up through it for ventilation. Between the house and the barn, nearer the former, was what remained of the winter's woodpile. Next to the corrals was a large earthen pond containing overflow from the cistern. A couple of sheds and a privy rounded out the facilities. Not bad for a cow camp, I guess, especially considering that some main ranch headquarters had less, my tiny outfit included.

On first glance things looked almost completely peaceful. We couldn't locate a soul. Then we noticed a couple of horses grazing off to one side of and beyond the corrals. At first they had been out of sight behind one of the cottonwood trees beside the bunkhouse. As we watched, two more horses came into view, and we finally realized that all four animals wore saddles. They were some distance beyond the house.

"Those horses are loose," Ike announced somewhat needlessly.

Monte grunted. "Not only that, they've been that way awhile. They wouldn't be grazin' along like that otherwise."

I followed his gaze, squinting hard. The horses were an awfully long way off. It was all I could do just to tell they wore saddles. They did seem relatively undisturbed, however.

Suddenly I thought I saw some movement near the woodpile. Monte must have seen it too, for he was in the process of pointing that way when a shot rang out and stopped him.

He said, "The barn. The window in the near corner, this side of the big door. See it?"

A puff of smoke rose lazily skyward. Only a good pair of eyes might have spotted it before it dissipated, but then, most cowboys I have known are farsighted to begin with.

"Someone's pinned down behind the woodpile," Monte added.

Almost as he said it, a figure jumped up and ran toward the side of the barn farthest from that lone window from which the shot had just been fired. Whoever it was must have decided a chance had to be taken, for he was instantly exposed and receiving fire from the barn. Two shots boomed before he dove out of sight around the far corner of the barn. The horses out past the corrals hardly seemed to pay any attention.

"Swell shot," Monte remarked. "Too bad those fellows didn't figure that out an hour ago."

"You figure they've been behind that woodpile for an *hour*?" I asked.

He shrugged. "We've been hearin' shots about that long, haven't we? What d'you figure?"

I shook my head. I had no idea.

Ike said, "Who do you think is in the barn?"

"I dunno," Monte answered. "This is a crazy deal. So far, I've only heard one rifle, but that don't tell me much. Those are probably some of our boys behind the woodpile, but who knows who's in the barn."

I was looking at the ground in front of me, at the tracks we had been following all along—mule and horse tracks both. "I think I know who they might be, but what I don't understand is why aren't the boys behind the woodpile shooting back?"

Monte looked at me. "That's a good question. I can't answer it, unless they aren't armed."

I didn't think that altogether likely, but before I could say so another shot sounded and another puff of smoke lifted from the barn window.

Monte looked around nervously. "I don't like this. We're like sitting ducks here, and we're within range. I say we ride off to the left, come in from behind the barn."

Neither Ike nor I had any objection to this. Monte led the way at a fast trot.

In short order we were beyond view of the shooter's window and galloping toward the rear of the barn. There were no windows on the side of the barn that faced us, but as we swung toward the back of the structure we could see not only two more windows and a door but the man who had apparently just sprinted there from the woodpile around front, hugging the wall beside the door. As we drew closer, the man began waving to us. We pulled up. He seemed to want us to veer toward the windowless side of the barn nearest us.

"Can you tell who that is?" Ike asked Monte.

"No, but I'd say he's figured out about who we are. Maybe he's recognized our horses, I dunno."

We cantered rapidly in the direction indicated. While we were doing this, the man who had waved at us opened the door wide enough to slip through and disappeared inside. We reached the side of the barn and pulled up.

We were still trying to decide what to do next when we heard a little shriek from inside the barn, something like door hinges squeaking as a door swings open, someone yelling from out front, and quite suddenly hoofbeats. And then something flashed in front of us, coming around the corner of the barn. We had only a couple of instants to recognize a horse and rider, and apparently the rider didn't even have that to realize that we were blocking his way. I tried to rein my sorrel aside but knew as I did that a collision was unavoidable.

Good thing was the other horse had not gained full speed; its rider tried to rein away in the same direction I did, but the impact of a shoulder-to-shoulder collision between our mounts was at least not a full one. Even so, both horses went down and I found myself hitting the ground, somehow clear of the struggling animals and without a notion how I managed to avoid a flailing hoof to the head.

As I got to my feet I heard someone yelling, thought I heard running footsteps approaching, and saw that both Ike and Monte had dismounted their horses. My sorrel had gotten to his feet a few steps away, and nearby a dust-coated gray had just done the same. The other rider, apparently also thrown clear, was just trying to rise.

And then, as four men rounded the corner of the barn on foot and converged on the scene, I realized with a start who that other rider was.

It was the girl I had encountered on the roadside from Magdalena.

* * *

Seven grown men just stood there as the girl finished getting to her feet. She had lost her hat somewhere and her hair was disheveled, her clothes and one side of her face coated with dust. It seemed clear as she dusted herself off that she was the one who had been shooting from inside the barn.

A somewhat astounded Monte said, "My God, men, what is this deal?"

Before anyone could say a word, the girl suddenly darted toward her horse. The unexpectedness of it seemed to catch everyone off guard for at least an instant. It was almost all she needed. I must have been the closest one to her by the time she reached the horse and may have been the only one who could have gotten to her before she was mounted. Even then, she had already gathered up the gray's reins and had a foot in the stirrup when I managed to grab her by the belt of her chaps. The horse shied away just as I pulled at the belt, and the girl came flying backward into me. We went down together, her on top and flailing away as she fell. She wasn't very heavy, but her rear end landed square in the middle of my stomach at about the same time as my back hit the ground. My wind whooshed out and all of a sudden I didn't care a whit if she got away again or not. I was just too desperate to get a breath to even pay attention to the fact that she had scrambled right back up and probably would have made it to her horse again if Monte and a couple of other men had not reached her first.

Two of them had her, one by each arm, by the time I was able to catch my breath enough again to sit upright. She was kicking wildly at Monte, who was doing a trifle awkward job of trying to grab her by the feet. Presently he managed to accomplish that task, however, and they wound up holding her in the air, still trying to kick and screaming for them to let her go.

"My God, what a she-cat! Someone get a rope!"

Someone actually did, and within minutes they had bound her hand and foot. It seemed the only way to contain her.

Of the six men there besides myself, I knew only Monte,

Ike, and one other. It just so happened that the other fellow I knew was the outfit's foreman. His name was Frank Baker. He had flowing white hair and a well-trimmed gray mustache that were accented by a leathery complexion and bright blue eyes. I figured his age as being somewhere between fifty-five and sixty, but I knew him to be as active as many men thirty years younger.

With the girl at least temporarily quieted, he viewed Monte, Ike, and me seriously for the first time. "Well, I guess you boys showed up just about right. She might've got away just like her friends if she hadn't run into the three of you."

Monte laughed. "It was Kel she ran into. Square on. Lucky someone didn't get hurt."

Frank Baker extended a hand my way. "Good to see you again, Kel. What're you doin' in the company of these two deadheads?"

I smiled, but my eyes were mostly on the girl. I had not missed Baker's mention of "her friends" who had got away. I said, "It's not just an everyday story, Frank. I figure you and I have notes to compare."

He followed my gaze quizzically. "Hmmm. Well, I reckon that sounds interesting enough. Let's go on up to the house. Somebody put up the horses and catch those out past the corrals. And somebody else bring the girl. I sure do wanta know what *she* has to say about all of this."

Those of us not assigned to tend to the horses trooped on over to the bunkhouse, where I noticed someone had spilled flour all over the porch. Two men had untied the girl's feet and either led or dragged her along behind us. Someone else had found her rifle, a .44-40 Winchester, lying beside a half-empty box of shells near the window inside the barn. She must have been surprised in the act of starting to reload, because the rifle had been found empty of ammunition. The girl was completely silent as she was led inside and made to sit down on a chair beside the long dinner table at the cookshack end of the bunkhouse, the rope still binding her arms to her sides.

On the far end of the room I noticed a food safe, doors swung open. Several cabinet doors located near the cook stove were also open. Shelves were all but empty in each case.

Frank Baker said, "You've seen this girl before, Kel? Your story have something to do with her?"

We sat around the table near the girl and I told them all about it, just as I had done with Monte and Ike earlier. Frank wagged his head in disbelief.

I said, "Now your story, Frank." I had watched the girl almost exclusively while I talked. She hardly batted an eye at anything I said. "What happened here?"

"Well, we rode up on your mule thieves, Kel. Don't seem no doubt about it. Found part of 'em busy ransacking the house and loading food and supplies on one of the mules, and part of 'em down at the barn doing I don't know what."

"My mules aren't pack animals, Frank," I said. "They didn't wear packsaddles."

Frank peered at me. "Oh, yeah? Well, the one I saw did. I reckon that's something we better check out at the barn. May have been *our* packsaddles those mules were wearing."

I looked at the girl. She seemed mildly irritated by the discussion, but that was about all.

The foreman went on. "I dunno how they managed to let us get so close without seeing us. There were ten of us, coming in from the west. I guess for the most part we had the house between us and them, and maybe they were in just such a hurry ransacking the place they forgot to keep an eye out. Anyhow, we were within a quarter of a mile away when someone spotted activity. We didn't think much about it, even then; just reckoned some of the boys had got here before us. But when we got within mebbe two hundred yards and were coming up out of the big swale that runs just west of the house, I guess they finally saw us. Before we realized anything was wrong, there were shots. We spread out and rushed 'em, and they scattered like quail. All but this girl here wound up fannin' it for the mountains to the south. For some reason she wound up in the barn, where I guess her horse was. Six of our boys took off after the bunch that ran, and in the melee the girl got the rest of us pinned down behind the woodpile between the house and the barn. We saw she was a girl when she ran in there and just couldn't bring ourselves to fire on her. We figured maybe she'd finally run out of ammunition, but after an hour and no sign of that happening we finally decided someone had to take a chance and get behind her and flush her out. That's about when you fellows showed up, I reckon."

I asked, "How many of them were there, Frank? Could you tell?"

"Five, counting the girl. Four that got away. They had no fewer than three pack animals with 'em. At least that's what they looked like to me; I guess now they were your three saddle mules, Kel."

I turned on the girl. "You people waylaid me, busted me over the head, and left me for dead—all for those three *mules*?"

At first I thought she was going to remain unresponsive. But finally she shrugged. "I didn't do anything to you."

"You told me your horse was lame. You distracted me while one of your friends sneaked up behind me. You call that nothing?"

"I did none of that. Believe me or not, I don't care."

I stared at her in disbelief. Suddenly I realized something was different about her. I wasn't sure what. She was the same girl, I was certain of that. Her face, her hair, her voice, her gray horse, her clothing.... The only thing I could think of was she had worn a vest earlier and now wore none. Was everything else the same? Chaps, breeches, shirt ... ? She no longer had a hat, although she could have lost that somewhere. But she was the same girl; I just knew I couldn't be wrong about that.

And then I remembered something else. "I told you earlier that I thought I had seen you somewhere before today. Do you deny that?"

She looked quite genuinely as if she didn't know what I was talking about. Then, in a flash, memory finally served me. At Magdalena the night before, when I first rode in on the way to my friend's house. I had noticed two men and a girl lounging in front of a store on the east side of town. I had gotten a reasonably good look at them but had paid them only passing attention. I'd noticed only that the girl was wearing man's attire and that she was pretty and that the two men were big and wore black, bushy beards and slouch hats. They had seemed to eye me as I passed. That was it, where I'd seen them. They may even then have been taking stock of my mules but probably had not seen where I had gone with them for the night. Then I realized that later on, when I had been drinking for some time inside one of the saloons, I had found myself telling the man next to me at the bar that I was headed for the Blue River to sell my three mules, that I would be setting out again in the morning. I guess I had even bragged some about how good the mules were and how I would be making good money when I sold them. And standing next to the man I was talking to had been a man with a black, bushy beard, a man who could easily have overheard everything I said.

Well, that drunk I put on must have been a swell one for me to have forgotten all of that. But it explained a lot, at least about how they had been able to plan ahead to waylay me.

I turned to Frank Baker. "This is the girl. The big man with the beard I told you about—him, the girl, and one other were in Magdalena last night. I know they are the same ones. Whoever hit me from behind and whoever the fifth rider you saw was, I have no idea. But this *is* the girl."

Frank shook his head. "Well, if this ain't one hell of a deal, I never saw one."

"What're we gonna do with her?" Monte asked.

The old foreman stroked his chin thoughtfully. "I dunno. I guess for starters we'll have to wait and see if the boys come back with any or all of her partners. Either way, I expect the sheriff in Socorro will have some interest in her. It'll just be a matter of gettin' her there, is all."

Monte didn't look satisfied. "What'll we do with her just *now* is what I was gettin' at. What'll we do with her tonight? She sure as hell can't be kept in this bunkhouse, with maybe two dozen cowhands due in and expectin' to bunk here."

"Hmmm. I hadn't thought about that."

"We can lock her in the tack room down at the barn," Ike suggested from across the table. "Ain't no windows there. No way she could get out."

Frank leveled a studied gaze on the girl. "Yeah, I suppose we could do that. Only I'd feel better if she was also kept under guard. You got a bedroll, girl?"

For the first time her expression showed strain. I even thought I detected a slight quiver in her upper lip. Nonetheless her voice was steady as she said, "Yes, I have a bedroll. It's on my saddle. And don't worry, I am very accustomed to it. I haven't slept on anything else for some while now."

For a moment Frank hardly seemed to know what to say. He looked at me, then back at the girl. "You know, young lady, you're as pretty as a spring flower and can't be a day over eighteen, yet you're about as strange a one as I've ever run across. Seems to me the least you could do is tell us your name and what on earth you're doing running with a crummy bunch of thieves such as ran off and left you here."

She sighed. "My name is Etta. I'm afraid that is about all I can tell you, except I'm sorry about the mules and the things we took here. I truly am sorry."

Frank only stared at her. So did the rest of us. There was just no way any of us knew what to make of her.

After a moment she straightened uncomfortably against the back of her chair and the rope that bound her arms. "If you don't mind, could I please have something to eat before you lock me up in the barn?"

CHAPTER 4

WITHIN the hour the six riders who had chased the mule thieves came riding into camp empty-handed. They said they had lost their quarry on a steep, timbered slope of the mountains. More than a few shots had been exchanged between the two parties. But when the four being chased had split into pairs and gone off in two separate directions, the six pursuers had soon lost both trails on rugged ground.

"Even the pack mules they had with them didn't slow them down much," one of the men, a fellow named Whitey Cameron told us. "And our horses were starting to give out from climbing hills. I'm sure they'll get back together up there somewhere, but it'd have been hell picking up their trail again this late in the day. What happened here? Where's the one who hid in the barn?"

Frank Baker told them about the girl. She was locked in the tack room as Ike had suggested, under guard, and still refused to tell us anything about herself or her companions.

What had been discovered down at the barn was that the thieves had indeed stolen three good packsaddles plus a sack full of grain. At the house several shelves filled with food intended for the roundup crew had been emptied. Fortunately enough had been left for the men to get by on until the roundup cook and chuck wagon were scheduled to arrive the following day.

"We've never locked up a thing around here," Frank Baker told me. "And this is the first time we've had anything more'n a meal or so—which we do not begrudge anyone—taken."

"What are you going to do about it?" I asked.

He made a somewhat hopeless gesture. "Not much I can do, Kel. Like Whitey said, those fellows would be hell to smoke out of those mountains. Besides, we've got a big cow works about to take place here. No way I can spare a crew of men to go after those thieves now, especially for no more than they took from us."

"And the girl?"

He thought about this. "What can I do? Send a couple of fellows down to Socorro with her, I suppose. Have her taken to the sheriff and the whole thing reported. Most likely, nothing will ever come of it as far as the ones who got away, but I don't know what else to do."

I nodded reluctantly in agreement. Somehow I hated to see the girl turned over to the law. Little telling what would be done to her, but I disliked the thought of it, nevertheless.

"What about you, Kel? Those mules of yours were probably the biggest loss taken. What are you gonna do about that?"

I shook my head. "I wish I knew. I had in mind tracking them down and getting my mules back. But now I don't know. Maybe I'll think on it tonight and decide something."

By sundown almost a dozen more men had shown up at the camp, some of them coming in twos and threes, as Monte had predicted they would. One group drove before them a remuda of extra horses to be used during the roundup.

I got to thinking about the girl locked in the tack room inside the barn. If I could just get her to talk, maybe I could learn where those friends of hers were headed with my mules.

After supper I told Frank and Monte, "I'd be glad to spell whoever you've got guarding the girl. I was sort of expecting to spread out my bedroll down at the barn for the night anyway. No use me taking up a bunk needed for one of the outfit's own here."

"It's up to you, Kel," Frank said. "There are two men down there now. You're welcome either place."

Monte's expression was perceptive. "It's sure strange how that girl wouldn't tell us anything, ain't it, Kel? Stranger yet how quick that bunch was to run off and leave her behind. You thinking to try again to get her to talk?"

"I'm hoping it might be worth a try," I said.

He seemed a bit hesitant with his next question. "Don't get me wrong about this, Kel, but are you figuring to stay down there alone with that girl tonight?"

I swiveled a little in my chair so I could look at him straight on. I said sincerely, "As God is my witness, Monte, I never thought of it that way. I was only—"

"I know, I know. I was just thinking to offer you some company down there if you wanted it. Things might look a little better, is all. I've got a bedroll on my saddle too, and I don't mind one bit sleeping on it."

"Thanks, Monte. I reckon it would be the best thing, all right. Sure you don't mind?"

He shrugged. "I never sleep well in a bunkhouse anyhow. Can't stand the close quarters or other men snoring and talking in their sleep. How about you, Ike—wanta stay down at the barn tonight?"

Ike was sitting on down the table from us, talking to some other fellows. He turned. "How's that? The barn? Naw, not me. Got a little poker game shaping up here. You go ahead."

Monte turned back to me. "I might watch a little of that. If you want, why don't you go on down and relieve those other two fellows so they can come up here and get some supper. I'll follow along in a little while."

This suited me fine. As a matter of fact, the idea had occurred to me that the girl might very well be easier to talk to when there wasn't a crowd around. I dismissed myself and headed on down to the barn.

Only the faintest trace of daylight remained as I stepped outside. Away from the bunkhouse windows, what real light there was came from a shiny-white crescent moon that was already well up in the sky. A dim glow of lantern light shone through the barn's lone front window, from which the girl had held off four men earlier.

I passed the woodpile and neared my destination. So I wouldn't surprise anyone, I rapped sharply on the big barn door before swinging it open partway. Two men lounged on the floor against a horse stall. Saddles lay all around—one of them, I could see, was mine. Inside, the light of a single lantern illuminated the barn's main interior. My horse, along with several others, had been put in one of the corrals out back. A door to a room just to my left was closed, but lantern light shone between the planks in the wall.

I had met both of the men only a couple of hours earlier. Their names were Jess and Bill.

"Things look quiet enough here," I said. "You fellows want a break?"

Neither man looked as if he needed to be asked twice. Jess said, rising, "We was beginning to think old Frank was gonna leave us down here without any supper."

Bill got to his feet alongside Jess. "Helluva duty, this. Guardin' a damn fool girl who has to be shut up inside a saddle shed."

"Well, you're in luck," I told them, walking over to take a look at the tack room door. It had a sliding wooden latch that could not be operated from the inside. "You check on the girl lately?"

" 'Bout a half hour ago," Jess replied. "Don't worry, she can't go nowhere. Nothin' in there but her, some bridles hangin' on the wall, a couple of packsaddles those thieves left behind, and a few odds and ends. No chance she can get out." He paused, then added with a wink, "One thing about it, though: She's a pretty one. Take a blind man to deny that."

"Yeah," I said. "Pretty like poison larkspur, maybe."

I watched them leave and turned back toward the tack room. I knocked lightly before releasing the latch, but did not pull the door open.

When there was no reply, I asked, "Are you awake?"
"Who is it?"
"Kel O'Day."
This was greeted with dead silence.
"The fellow with the mules," I explained. "The one you robbed."
"Oh . . ."
"Can I come in?"
"Suit yourself," she said resignedly. "Seems to me you have the latch on your side anyway."

I opened the door. The girl knelt on the floor, seemingly busy untying the strings that bound her bedroll. A few feet away lay her saddle, which someone must have brought to her after her horse had been turned loose in one of the corrals.

Overhead, a low-burning kerosene lantern hung by its bail from a hook in the ceiling; it could be reached to adjust its light from the floor, which was earthen, hard-packed. The place smelled strongly of leather. Bridles and hackamores hung on one wall, just as Jess had described. The two packsaddles sat atop a rail built for that purpose and extending across the room on my left. Neither of the packsaddles looked to be in top condition. The thieves probably had taken the best ones available.

The girl finished untying her bedroll and unrolled it with a flip of the hand. Then she turned toward me.

"Well, what do you think of my quarters? Pretty fancy, huh?"

"Look," I said, feeling very awkward and even a bit guilty. "I'm sorry about this. But you did bring it mostly on yourself. Surely you know that."

She shrugged. "Maybe I did, maybe I didn't. Sometimes we do things whether we like them or not."

She rose, hefted her saddle by its fork, and swung it onto the rail behind one of the packsaddles. She then very carefully made sure the cinches were swung atop the saddle so that nothing dangled as far as the floor. I could see that she was no stranger to anything she was doing.

She had already removed her chaps, and these too she lay atop the saddle.

"I'd offer you a chair," she said, "but as you can see I'm a bit short on furniture at the moment."

I looked around and spotted a couple of nail kegs sitting in one corner of the room, one atop the other. I walked over to them and found both empty. They seemed sturdy enough, and after checking them out for spiders I offered one to the girl. I sat the other one on end in front of the door for me. About fifteen feet separated us.

"Thanks," she said after a moment's appraisal of her keg. She seemed tired as she sat down. "I guess I shouldn't be short with you. After all, you were the one who was wronged. Is this a social call or what?"

For a moment I just looked at her. She had this way about her of keeping a person off balance. As Frank Baker had before me, I guessed her age at about eighteen. She acted more like twenty-five. I figured I'd had more than an average amount of schooling for my day, but this girl actually appeared educated. She certainly didn't look like one to consort with thieves.

"Well?" she asked. "Are you just going to sit there and stare at me?"

"You said we sometimes do things whether we like them or not," I finally managed. "I assume that includes helping your friends steal my mules and then holding these cowhands here off while the rest of your gang got away. Are you saying you were forced into doing those things?"

Her smile was barely that. "What difference does it make to you?"

"Well, maybe not a lot. Maybe I'm just curious why you won't tell me anything about yourself and your friends—where they might be going with my mules, for example."

She sighed. "I told you I was sorry about that. Do those mules mean that much to you?"

"At least that much," I said.

She eyed me quizzically. "Three mules? Three lousy mules?"

I nodded. "It's not so much the principle of the thing, it's the money. What they cost me. The profit I was going to make when I sold them."

"You're serious, aren't you?"

"Tolerably."

"I see." She seemed to be trying to figure me out, which suited me just fine, since I was having the same problem with her. "Are you a cowhand? Do you ride for this outfit?"

"No, not this outfit," I said. "But I've ridden for several around here. Just now, I've got a small place of my own on the west side of the San Mateos—a few cows, a section of land, a roof over my head. Nothing much to brag about and sure no money in it, at least not yet."

"Which is why you were going into the mule business?"

I shrugged. "I sold a small bunch of steers and had some cash in my pocket when I came across a chance to put it to use. May not seem like a lot to some people, but it was a pretty big deal to me. Probably mean whether or not I make it through another year on my place." This last was something of an exaggeration, although not as much so as I would have liked.

The girl looked away—sadly, I thought.

I said, "I'm going to be your guard for the rest of the night. Me and another fellow, who'll be down later."

Her eyes met mine, this time perhaps a bit suspiciously. "Oh?"

I sighed and leaned forward. "Look, I would've stayed in the barn tonight no matter what. I volunteered to relieve your guards so I could talk to you. All I want are my mules back before they're galled by packsaddles or crippled and ruined on the rocks somewhere. I was hoping somehow to learn where your friends were headed. Surely they made some provision for getting back together with you. I mean, when they escaped from here and left you behind . . . you at least knew how you might find them again, didn't you?"

She wagged her head from side to side. "I told you before I can't tell you anything about that. I'm sorry. I wish none of this had ever happened. I wish I could help you and I wish you could help me. I'm sorry."

I said, "The foreman of this outfit is going to send you to Socorro tomorrow. You'll be turned over to the sheriff there. I don't know if anything much will happen to you over it, but it seems to me that somewhere along the line you're going to have to say what's what and who's who in this deal."

Somehow I wasn't surprised when she didn't respond. She simply looked away again, this time with a lightly troubled expression on her face.

"Well," I said, getting to my feet, "if you change your mind, I'll be just outside. Or if you need anything. I'm sorry you've got no better place than this to sleep."

She smiled wanly. "Thank you."

I closed the door behind me and fastened the latch. Then I walked over to get the lantern. It hung from a peg sticking out from a post on one side of a horse stall. I lifted it off the peg and went over to locate my saddle and bedroll from among those scattered around on the floor.

I wondered where Monte was, but didn't worry much about him. He would probably be along soon enough.

I didn't carry a pocket watch, but I calculated it was about nine o'clock. I felt tired. I located my saddle and removed my bedroll. Then I went back over to the horse stall, replaced the lantern on its peg, and proceeded to spread my bedroll out on the floor. I turned the lantern down low, took off my boots and hat, and lay down.

I didn't really intend to fall asleep until Monte got there. I wasn't sure how necessary it might be, but I supposed one of us ought to stay awake just to make sure nothing happened with the girl. Nonetheless, I was so tired I must have dozed off, because the next thing I knew I was coming awake with a start.

At first I had no idea what had awakened me. I only knew that I found myself sitting upright and trying to focus my eyes. The light was dim, but I sensed that someone was in the barn with me. And then I saw someone standing just inside the main barn door, a slight figure that proceeded to step toward me and in a second had come far enough into the light that I could see who it was.

For a moment I fully doubted my senses. But then I knew I couldn't be mistaken and I was sure I wasn't dreaming. It was the girl, only now she was wearing that vest again as well as her chaps and hat. Instinctively I glanced toward the tack room door. It was closed, the sliding latch seemingly in place just as I had left it, and faint lantern light still shone between the cracks in the wall.

I said "What the hell . . . ?" and started to get to my feet. But even before I got to my knees I realized that someone else was there. A quick flash of movement to my left—coming from the other side of the horse stall—caught my eye and caused me to stop.

Too many things happened at once then, most of them frighteningly familiar. A man with a black beard stood to my left, no more than ten feet away. He had a six-gun in his right hand. Then there was a noise behind me, and as I started to turn I noticed that the girl had moved toward the tack room door.

That's all I got to see, because for the second time in a day something struck me on the back of the head, and whatever was still functioning normally inside my poor brain was replaced by a bright flash of light, a burst of mind-numbing pain, then darkness.

CHAPTER 5

IF it had been a dream, I would have been glad to wake up from it. That way my head would quit hurting. As it was, the pain only grew worse as consciousness returned.

I heard a voice. It was Monte's. "Dammit, Kel, can you hear me? C'mon, wake up. What happened?"

I opened my eyes with the unhappy knowledge that I had been through this before. At least the blurriness cleared quickly this time. I was lying on my back, looking at the ceiling of the barn. Monte knelt over me, one hand under my neck, I suppose in an attempt to hold my head off the ground. Low lantern light flickered against the ceiling. Best I could tell, it was still dark outside.

"Am I . . . bleeding?" I asked sluggishly, trying to feel for the back of my head at the same time.

"I don't think so. But if you keep this up we're gonna have to change your name to Knothead. You've got a bump back there the size of a pullet egg."

I groaned as my fingers encountered the knot. Monte wasn't exaggerating a bit.

"Do you remember what happened?"

"Yeah, sort of," I said, struggling to sit up. "Somebody clubbed me again. And if you can believe this, I think it was that same bunch of somebodies that did it the first time!"

"I can believe it," he said ruefully. "The girl's gone. They must have opened up the tack room and let her out after they did their little job on you."

My gaze had settled on the tack room door. It was ajar, and the latch was slid back. The lantern still burned low inside.

I said, "It's funny you'd say it that way—that they let her out 'after' they knocked me cold. As a matter of fact, she was already out. I know because I saw her. She stood right over there and was walking toward the tack room when I got hit."

Monte seemed puzzled. "Why would she be doing that—if she was already out?"

I wagged my head slowly. There was more to it, if I could just remember.

Monte asked, "How did they get in here without you seeing them?"

"I fell asleep waiting for you. I didn't aim to . . . I guess I was just too tired. Something woke me up later. I saw the girl, then one of the fellows with a black beard, and *wham*! That's it."

Monte looked contrite. "Dammit, I'm sorry, Kel. I got to watchin' that card game and the next thing I knew I was sittin' in for just a few hands. You know how hard it is to sit in on a card game for just a few hands."

I nodded and asked, "What time is it?"

"After midnight, I reckon. One o'clock, mebbe even two. Dammit, I am sorry, Kel. I got to winnin' and, aw hell, you know how it is."

My head hurt too much for me to argue a point like that. "Never mind. You had no way of knowing those characters would come back. Maybe we all should have been more worried about that happening, but that's easy to say now."

He seemed happy enough to accept this, but looked thoughtful as he said, "I still don't figure it. If the girl was already loose when you woke up, why were they still hangin' around?"

I was looking once again at the tack room door, recalling now what I couldn't remember a while ago. "Just before I was hit, that door was still closed and the latch was forward. I know it was."

Monte stared at me. "I don't get it."

"The girl was out already, standing right over there, just inside the main door. She started walking toward me, then turned toward the tack room. The door was latched; I swear it." I paused. "How was it when you got here?"

"Well, I reckon it was just like it is now. I saw that even before I located you. Both lanterns were still burnin' low. I went over and looked inside without so much as touchin' the door. When I seen the girl was gone, I looked around and saw you stretched out on the floor. I came straight over to see if I could bring you around, and that's all I've done. No one else even knows about what happened yet."

"But doesn't it strike you as strange, what I said?"

"Well, yeah, but I don't know enough to make anything out of it. I mean, what—?"

I interrupted him. "Let me tell you something else. Do you remember how I described the girl to you when you first came across me at the windmill after they had taken my mules? Do you remember I said she wore a hat and a vest? Well, she wasn't wearing either one when we next saw her, right outside the barn here. I figured she could have lost the hat and done nearly anything with the vest. Do you remember that?"

Monte nodded in assent, but he clearly didn't see what I was getting at.

"This time she was wearing both the hat and the vest. I have no idea where they came from. It was as if she wasn't even the same girl."

For a long moment Monte just looked at me. Finally he said, "Friend Kel, I think maybe you've had one too many thumps on the head for one day. I sure do!"

"I'm only telling you what I saw."

He looked contemplative. "Well, whatever you say. But I reckon it don't make much difference now. They're gone, the girl and whoever else was here. And I don't see a thing we can do about it just now. What say we go on up to the house and get a cup of coffee? Do you feel up to it? Won't be long till time for breakfast, and I'm sure Frank Baker will wanta know what's happened here."

He helped me to my feet, and other than the pain in my

head I suppose you could say I felt all right. At least I wasn't dizzy, and I could walk unassisted.

We doused the lanterns in the barn and went on up to the house.

"I'm going after them," I stated flatly to Frank and Monte an hour later over my fourth steaming hot cup of coffee. "Soon as it's light enough to read their tracks, I'm going. I want my mules back, and I figure I owe someone a couple of cracks on the head by now. It's as simple as that."

It was almost 4 A.M. Monte had been wrong about the time by at least an hour. The roundup crew was already stirring from its bunks; a couple of the men assigned temporary cook duty were up and working on breakfast at the big cookstove behind us. Daylight would find them at the corrals catching their horses to begin the cow works. It would find me there too, looking to saddle my sorrel cow pony, although for an entirely different reason.

Frank and Monte had been trying to explain to me what little luck I was likely to have going after the mule thieves.

"I can understand how you feel, boy," Frank said. "But what real chance do you have? Even if you catch up to them, there's still only you against several. And from the sounds of things, they're likely a bad bunch to mix with. You'd need help, which I'd gladly send with you, except you know my situation here. I just can't spare the men it'd take. I really can't."

I said, "I understand that, Frank. And I wouldn't expect you to. But I'm still going."

Someone came stumbling past on his way to the door leading outside. It was Ike, still half-asleep and his business clearly of an urgent nature. He went out the door without a word.

Monte said, "Dammit, Frank, I feel kind of responsible. If I hadn't took a hand in that card game—"

"You're probably right about that," Frank interrupted

sternly, but then half-smiled. "Although it's also possible what we'd have now is *two* men with bumps on their heads instead of just one!" He laughed lightly at his own words.

Monte was unfazed. "What I'm thinkin' is if you can't spare a whole crew to go with Kel, what about just a couple of us?"

Frank peered at him. "You and Ike, I suppose."

"Well, I can't really speak for Ike, but I'm sure he'd go."

The foreman nodded thoughtfully. "I see. Get our pack-saddles back too, would you?"

"Why, sure. Kel don't need 'em. He's already said his mules aren't pack animals."

"And some of our other stuff, if there's anything left of it?"

"Well, yeah . . ."

"And all the while you'd be on the outfit's payroll, right?"

"Well . . ."

Frank continued to look thoughtful. "I dunno, Monte, I dunno."

"Aw, c'mon, Frank—"

Suddenly the door flew open and Ike stepped back inside. The look on his face must have been what caused Monte to stop in midsentence. He looked at us as if he hadn't noticed any of us there when he'd gone out only a few minutes earlier.

"What's the deal? I thought you two were down at the barn. And what're those horses doin' loose outside? I thought we penned everything for the night."

Frank exchanged glances with Monte and me, then looked back at Ike. "Horses, Ike? Loose?"

"I ain't been drinkin' and I don't think I've just been dreamin'," Ike declared simply.

Frank frowned.

"All I did was step out back to take a pee," Ike went on, "and I jumped two horses grazin' by the cellar. It's still dark and I didn't notice a thing till one of 'em snorted. Like to scared me right outa my boots, let me tell you. They trotted off lickety-split and disappeared in the dark. Then, when I came back around the corner of the house, I heard a horse whinny. I looked around and could just make out a couple more standin' between here and the barn. Both of 'em was light-colored or I wouldn't have seen either one."

Frank looked a quick question at me and Monte. Monte said, "It was dark as pitch when we came across from the barn, Frank. Even that slip of a moon had gone down. We never saw any horses. You know we'd have said if we did."

Frank seemed to accept this, his mind going on quickly to his next thought. "You have any idea how long it's been since those fellows konked you on the head, Kel?" he asked.

I shrugged. "Hours, I guess."

"You don't suppose . . ."

"What d'you mean konked him on the head?" Ike wanted to know. "Who—?"

Frank ignored him. "I think we better take a look down at the corrals."

Which we did. The corrals were empty. My friends the mule thieves must have let down the gates, hoping of course to avoid, or at least delay, pursuit. And with first light of day, over two dozen grumbling cowboys were out on foot trying to round up as many animals as they could that hadn't already wandered too far afield to be caught.

We managed to spread out and surround four horses found grazing a short way beyond the corrals. We hazed them back through the nearest corral gate and gathered around to observe our catch. We weren't long in agreeing that the situation had some real peculiarities.

As strange as anything was the fact that all four of these horses bore brands none of us had ever seen before. Not a one of them belonged in the outfit's remuda. Too, it was evident that each horse had rolled in the dust since last being ridden, but three of them still showed clearly the sweat marks of saddles recently worn. More curious yet, two of the horses were light grays (probably the ones Ike had seen near the barn a short while before), and seen apart, could easily have been mistaken one for the other. I was certain one of them had been ridden by the girl who had collided with me and my sorrel the evening before. I was not at all certain about the other one.

None of the horses were in good flesh, and the three that exhibited the fresher saddle marks looked to have been ridden hard.

As the sun peeked over the Magdalena Mountains, we began to spot other horses scattered in small bunches out across the plains. Most, if not all, had strayed far enough away that rounding them up any way but horseback would almost certainly prove impossible.

Frank Baker shook his head in disgust. "On top of everything else, looks like someone made a little swap while they were here last night. Even if we gather every horse that was turned out here, I'll lay odds we'll still be missin' at least four that were ours."

Monte stood beside me, also eyeing the horses. "They probably rode the legs off those old ponies when they came back for the girl. Thought they needed fresh horses, on top of puttin' us on foot."

"And to think these are the only ones we caught," someone else said. "Ain't that swell!"

Frank shrugged. "That don't surprise me none. Horses are like folks: Most times they'd rather hang around with chums than with strangers. And these animals were tired; probably didn't much care about gallopin' off with those ponies of ours. Just hung around here, grazin' a little and restin' up. We're damn lucky we had even them to catch, is what I say."

"My mules . . ." I said suddenly. "What did they do with my mules while all this was going on?"

Monte looked at me. "They probably left them somewhere up in the hills, Kel. Wouldn't be no reason for them to drag the mules along. No tellin' where the thieves *or* the mules are by now."

I was looking at the two gray horses, recalling my confusion about the girl of just a few hours earlier. Certainly there was no less confusion now.

Ike was saying from nearby, "I still can't believe it, Kel. They clubbed you over the head again?"

I passed a hand over the back of my head. "Carry a knot like the one I've got here, and you'll believe it, Ike."

Monte was looking at Frank Baker. "Well, what are we gonna do, boss?"

"Why, choose four men to saddle up and go after the other horses, I reckon. What else?"

No one said anything, and Frank looked at me. "Your sorrel is gone with the rest of 'em, Kel. And I remember how in a hurry you were to take off after them mule thieves. Question is: Can you give me time first to get as many of our animals back as we can? If you wanta go ahead, I'll give you the best of these four here and we'll make do with the other three. If you wait, I'll make sure you're well mounted and provisioned, even if we don't bring in your sorrel. What's more, I'm just about mad enough at that bunch of whatnots now to let Monte and Ike go with you. What say?"

I looked around at what at the time just might have been the best overall crew of cowhands in Socorro County, all standing and shuffling their feet and completely at loose ends without horses to ride. I looked at Monte and Ike, both of whom seemed eager to help me recover my mules. And then I looked back at those two gray horses, thinking about the girl, who had begun to seem like a different person each time I saw her. . . .

Finally I said, "Sure, Frank. I'll wait. Fact is, I'll even volunteer to help go after the horses. But after that, the sooner I get on the trail of those mule thieves the better."

CHAPTER 6

MY head hurt and I'd had no sleep and Frank Baker might have had some age on him but he damned sure wasn't slow of mind or unobservant. Frank sent me up to the house to get some rest while four other fellows saddled up to do the horse wrangling.

By about noon, when I'd slept what seemed half a life away, I was back up and about and on my way down to discover that about forty horses were back in the corrals where they belonged. Twenty or so were still unaccounted for, but everyone seemed happy just to see the ones that were there. A day of the roundup had already been lost and no one wanted to think about losing another day. A search for the remaining horses would be started by a dozen cowboys on fresh mounts later that afternoon. In the meantime, Monte, Ike, and I went down to pick out the animals we would ride in pursuit of the mule thieves. To my chagrin, my Slant K sorrel was not among those brought in.

Monte told me, "Frank says take your pick among what's here. I'll let you know if you're about to stake claim to somebody's favorite animal."

I picked out a lanky chestnut that looked like he might make a good mountain traveler, while Ike and Monte shook out loops for a bay and a sorrel respectively. Apparently I had not selected anybody's favorite mount. As a sort of afterthought I asked what my companions thought of taking the fresher of the two grays left by the mule thieves along as a packhorse.

"Maybe Frank would loan us that old packsaddle I saw last

night in the barn," I said. "And a tarp. I'm sure there's an extra one or two of those around somewhere."

Monte eyed the two grays skeptically. Both still bore sweat marks from the morning's use and stood just across the corral from us. "Up to you, Kel. If you wanta ask, don't see why Frank would care."

I wasn't sure why I did either, except there was no telling how long or how far this chase would take us, and depending on how many provisions Frank Baker could actually spare, I meant to go as well prepared as possible. I only figured to pick one of the grays to save on the outfits' already depleted remuda.

As expected, Frank had no problem with us taking the packhorse, saddle, and a tarp. In about an hour we were saddled up, outfitted—albeit sparingly—and ready to go.

Frank saw us off. "They probably went south toward the mountains again, but my guess is you'll have trouble pickin' up their trail in close here. Too many horse tracks have been laid around this place since last night. All I can say is, good luck. And be careful. Like I said before, that bunch could be bad business to tangle with. Ain't worth gettin' killed over."

I guess I hadn't considered *that* possibility before. It gave me something to think about as we rode south, let me tell you.

As Frank had predicted, we had little chance of picking up a trail anywhere close to the cow camp. Tracks were everywhere, coming and going.

Nevertheless, half a mile out we pulled up. Ahead of us were a group of tracks that seemed directed in a uniform pattern toward the mountains. They were the first we'd seen that fit such a description. Monte dismounted for a closer look.

"What d'you think," Ike asked, leaning forward with arms folded across his pommel.

"Hard to tell. These tracks could've been made last night; then again they could've been yesterday's."

"Could any of them be mule tracks?" I asked, assuming a pose similar to Ike's. I had never made any claims to being much of a tracker myself.

He shook his head. "Don't think so. Were any of your mules shod?"

"No. They were all barefoot."

"Well, all of these animals wore horseshoes. No barefoot mules in the lot."

"How many would you say?"

"Four, I think."

I straightened in my saddle. "That would be the right number at least. Wouldn't it?"

Monte shrugged. "You got me, Kel. Frank said he counted five riders yesterday, includin' the girl. But we only found four of their horses left behind this morning, and one of those was the girl's gray. Logic says they didn't bring the mules with 'em when they came back for the girl. Could be one of 'em stayed behind with the mules."

"Makes sense," Ike said.

Monte looked at me. "What say? You wanta follow 'em or not?"

"I don't see what else to do," I said. "It's the closest thing to a trail we've seen yet."

"I'd certainly agree with that," Ike said as Monte turned to remount his horse.

We followed those tracks for a mile farther, climbing a gradual foot slope that soon became thick with piñon and juniper. Steeper slopes rose before us and a good deal of climbing seemed imminent. The tracks we were following had led us slightly east from where we had first encountered them but were still going mostly south.

After a while we were on rocky ground and the tracks became less distinct. They had been made following a lightly used cow trail or we probably would have lost them altogether. We pulled up once again to discuss the situation.

I asked Monte, who once again had dismounted to take a better look, "See anything new? Still only four sets of tracks?"

He straightened. "Best I can tell, everything's still the same. They haven't met up with anyone else and they're holdin' steady as a summer breeze in the same direction they been goin' all day."

"Not doing much to hide their trail, either," I observed. "I wonder why."

Monte shrugged. "Maybe they weren't much worried about anybody comin' after 'em. After all, they did all they could to leave a whole camp full of cowhands on foot. And whoever's afraid of a cowboy chasin' anything down on foot!"

The tracking became more difficult yet over the next quarter mile or so. At least three times Monte thought he had lost the trail altogether, before finally finding a hoof mark just visible in crusted soil, or a rock recently scuffed by a horseshoe, or finally a pile of dung that could not be more than twelve or fifteen hours old and was probably much less.

We were not making good time and the afternoon shadows were growing long by the time we achieved the crest of a certain narrow ridge that gave us a great view of the country below and behind us but revealed only more trees and steep mountain slopes ahead. We were still following a trail of sorts, but now it was more of a deer trace than one used by cows. In addition to the several miles in horizontal distance we had achieved, I estimated we had already gained a thousand feet in elevation above the cow camp and were well beyond the areas where anybody's cows normally ranged. Matter of fact, except for a few miners and an occasional renegade Apache escaped from a reservation somewhere, not too many people found good or frequent reason to be where we were just then.

Once again, Monte was on the ground studying tracks. A fork in the trail seemed to be what had precipitated the action this time. One fork appeared to follow the ridge top toward higher ground, while the other swerved right toward a deep canyon that wound its way down out of the mountains to the northwest.

After a moment, Monte left his horse ground-reined and walked a few yards down the right-hand fork of the trail. At first he was simply watching the ground as if still tracking; then he got to looking thoughtfully off into the canyon. Presently he came shuffling back our way, spurs jingling and his brow deeply knit.

"Now what?" I asked. "Which way did they go?"

"That's the problem," he said. "They went both ways. Two to the right and two to the left. Don't ask me why, but it sure looks like they've split up."

Ike looked as if he had already surmised as much from Monte's actions. "Which way does that right fork go? In the canyon or around the hill?"

Indeed, a pine- and juniper-cloaked mountainside bordered the canyon on the north, around which the trail could conceivably go.

Monte shrugged. "Couldn't tell for sure, but I think it goes on around. Didn't look that way at first, from here, but now I'm not so sure."

"Well, I'll be damned," Ike said. "How do you figure it, Kel? Why'd they split up?"

I shook my head. "You got me." Then I added, "Are you sure, Monte? Two went each way?"

As if mostly to satisfy me, he turned and strode alongside the left fork of the trail for a ways, studying the ground carefully as he went.

Presently he stopped and looked back. "See for yourself if you want. Looks pretty clear to me. Two this way, and two that."

I was willing enough to take his word for it, but decided to get down and have a look just to see if I could tell anything on my own. The ridge top was composed generally of soft dirt and relatively fewer rocks than we had been encountering; the two sets of horse tracks in each fork of the trail were distinct.

"Okay," I said. "What do we do now?"

Monte's gaze was trained down the left-hand fork. "If we keep going that way I'm guessin' we'll wind up passin' through Monica Saddle. That would put us near the head of Bear Trap Canyon and only a tad short of Mount Withington. Now, not that the goin's all that easy, mind you, but whoever made these tracks could go just about any direction from Monica Saddle—on south especially, or southwest down Bear Trap Canyon. No tellin' about whoever took the right fork. They're bound to meet back up someplace, but who's to know when or where that might be."

I just looked at him. Monica Saddle lay approximately between the head of Monica Canyon—which ran almost due north from the mountains out onto the edge of the plains—and the upper reaches of Bear Trap Canyon, which angled off in a southwesterly direction. Mount Withington rose generally south of the saddle. The country all around was steep and tree-covered, and a mile's travel in such environs was the equal of two or three miles across flat country. It did not get less rugged as one went south.

Monty went on, "I reckon this could be some sort of trick to throw us off, but somehow I don't think so. My guess is, the girl and one other went on to someplace where they all plan to meet while the other two maybe went after the mules and whoever that fifth man Frank Baker saw yesterday was. I'm not sure why they'd do that, except maybe to save the girl a longer ride. In any case, I figure either trail oughta eventually lead us to the same place."

"So what do we do?" Ike asked from nearby. "Flip a coin?"

I was thinking about the girl again, about what Monte had said about her and "one other" going one way while the other two went another. I was also recalling the confusion I had experienced the night before when the girl had so strangely appeared right before I was hit over the head again. I was thinking about those things and only half listening when Monte's somewhat indecisive "Well . . ." was interrupted by a sudden movement from Ike. The latter had straightened in his saddle, his gaze a hard squint, cast southward beyond Monte and me.

Monte asked, "Well, what is it? What're you lookin' at?"

"Over there," he said, pointing. "Over there—on the side of that mountain."

We tried to follow his directions. Mountainsides were plentiful from where we stood.

Then we saw what he pointed at. A horse and rider poised statuelike in a small clearing perhaps a quarter of a mile away. Moments later a second rider appeared beside the first and became equally still.

Monte and I turned to mount our horses almost in unison. Monte was saying as he swung astride, "Do you figure they've seen us?"

"I'd nearly bet on it," Ike said, still squinting. "Fact is, I make it damn strange they're just sittin' there watchin' like they are—"

He never finished voicing his thought. A gunshot split the air from somewhere off to our right and a bullet ricocheted off a branch not ten feet in front of us. My horse shied almost out from under me and it was all I could do to keep my seat and hang on to the lead rope of the gray behind me. A second shot followed the first, and I had no idea where it hit.

Monte yelled, "Head for the trees, for chrissake! Get out of the open!"

I didn't need to be told twice. Even as Monte spoke, I was already spurring my chestnut toward the nearest cover, to my left. We hit the trees at a dead run and went crashing through brush that was over my head. Somehow I hung onto my hat but let go of the packhorse's lead rope. I could hear the gray crashing along behind us, nevertheless. Somehow I just assumed Monte and Ike were there, too. It was only after I had gone about two hundred yards and left the high part of the ridge we were on altogether that I realized they were not. I kept hearing shooting, and once I thought I heard more crashing in the brush well to my right and somewhat behind me. But then I was alone and knew it. I pulled up to listen. Another shot rang out, then another. I heard a yell from far off, but nothing else. I had no idea where Monte and Ike had gone.

I ventured farther along in the brush and trees, avoiding the steep side slopes of Monica Canyon to my left and going mainly south. Only once did I catch sight again of that small clearing where we had seen the two riders only minutes earlier. The clearing was empty, no sign at all of the two riders. The only thing I knew for sure was, the shots definitely had not come from their direction.

I waited for several minutes to see if Monte and Ike would show up, and when they did not I eased on southward without the foggiest notion what I was going to do next.

CHAPTER 7

FOR the life of me I couldn't figure out where Monte and Ike had gone. I was in thick timber with no one but my chestnut and the gray packhorse for company. The gray had stayed with me like a lost pup ready to accept anything that moved as its mama, but my two human companions had disappeared altogether. The shooting had stopped also. Except for my horses' heavy breathing and the thump-thump of my own heartbeat, it was as if all noise had ceased.

I had pulled up beneath a towering fir to listen and wait for some sign of my friends. I felt it foolish to call out to them, for I didn't know what had happened to them and was afraid that our attackers would still be within earshot of me. It would be just my luck for only the wrong person to hear or see me if I did anything stupid. I figured Monte and Ike were probably thinking the same thing, assuming they were alive and *able* to do anything at all.

This was a pretty sobering thought in its own right—that either or both of my friends might have been wounded or killed by the gunfire.

The sun was set now, and that same crescent moon I had seen the night before was well up in the sky. I calculated full dark would soon be upon me.

I thought of backtracking to the spot where I had last seen Monte and Ike, but I wasn't a bit sure I could find it again in poor light. After a few minutes more, I reined around and rode on, staying within heavy timber. The only thing I could think to do was find a place to camp somewhere reasonably distant from the place of attack, where I could wait for morning to do something about relocating my companions.

With the last light of day fading fast, I made my way to the bottom of a canyon. A tiny spring there seeped water into a fetid-looking pool. I wasn't sure I could bring myself to drink from it, but at least it would do for the horses. I removed their saddles and went about setting up camp for the night. Because of the circumstances, I would have no fire, no hot food, no coffee. A blanket for warmth, some beef jerky, and a can of peaches would just have to do. Tomorrow would surely bring a better day.

I awoke long before the sun found its way into the canyon, back sore and feeling little rested. Sleeping on the ground will do that to you; it's like every night in a strange bed.

I decided to risk a small fire and pot of the seep water for coffee. While this was boiling, I saddled my horses and chewed some more jerky. I was in a hurry to find Monte and Ike. And I certainly didn't want to lose any more time than necessary before resuming the search for my mules and whoever had taken them. Because I had little doubt the latter were some of those who had taken shots at us last night, my interest in catching up to them had grown into a full-fledged determination.

Sunshine was just beginning to bathe one side of the canyon when I mounted up a short while later. I found my tracks from the night before and decided to retrace them. Atop the canyon rim I found where I must have crossed rockier ground than I remembered, for I promptly lost the tracks. It had been just dark enough when I came that way that nothing looked very familiar in daylight.

I tried softer ground, leaving the canyon behind. North—I was sure I should go north to get back to where I last saw Monte and Ike.

I found a trail, lacking fresh tracks of any kind. Old deer tracks, and perhaps those of a coyote, were all I spotted. Across a narrow saddle, then a shallow canyon, I came to another trail. This time there were horse tracks, two sets, left by shod horses, going south. Whoever had passed by might very well have done so as recently as the night before. But that's about all I could tell. I just wished I was half as good a tracker as Monte.

It occurred to me that these tracks *could* have been Monte's and Ike's. Had they been unable to strike my trail and were wandering aimlessly as I was now, trying to find me?

It gave me pause. Which way to go? Back to where I had last seen my friends, or take a chance on these tracks? Considering the time it might take to go back, considering the fact I wasn't even sure I could find my way there, and because I had reasonably fresh tracks before me, I decided on the latter choice.

Even for such as me, the tracks weren't hard to follow. The trail rimmed a canyon and led generally southward. And even though thick timber was all around, the trail more than once led me into the open view of anyone who might lurk across the canyon. I kept my eyes peeled as I rode.

Soon the trail left the canyon in favor of a tree-covered ridge. It was atop this ridge that a second trail intersected the one I had been following. On it were more fresh tracks, only this time it looked like they were both coming and going. The tracks I had been following crossed the second trail apparently without pause, and were laid atop the most recent of the new tracks. Had I been a better tracker I'm sure I might have told more than I could about the timing of things. I was convinced that none of the tracks were very old, however, and it made me wonder.

If I was following Monte and Ike, why had they gone right on past the new trail? I figured if they had passed by in the dark they probably never knew about the tracks. But what bothered me was if it hadn't been Monte and Ike at all. . . .

Confused, I decided the only thing for me to do was stay with the trail I was following. It left the ridge and started off into another canyon toward the west.

The trail was winding and steep all the way to the bottom of the canyon. Mount Withington loomed behind me now. The tracks I was following indicated horses had been traveling at a much quicker pace than before. Then, after about half a mile, I came to a place where the riders had pulled off the trail, and it looked like they had dismounted in a grove of trees well hidden from almost any view. Fir needles covered the ground and nowhere could I find a clean boot print. Only disturbed duff, a couple of heel prints, and places where the fir needles were flattened—as if someone had sat or lay down to rest.

I had little idea how long they had stayed there, although I suspected some portion of the night. I did find where the horses had been tied nearby, dung heaps and disturbed ground enough to indicate at least an hour or even two. But there was certainly no sign of a campfire, so if it had been Monte and Ike, they must have entertained similar ideas to mine regarding being discovered. Yet why would they have come so far from where they had last seen me during the night? Why hadn't they waited as I did for daylight when they could at least look for a trail?

And then, where the horses had been tied, I quite by accident discovered a clean boot print. No way was it large enough to be Monte's or Ike's.

Something moved on a hillside a quarter of a mile down the canyon. I only caught a glimpse through the trees around me, but that was enough. Quickly I moved for a better view. A small opening in the hillside foliage revealed a horse and rider just before they slipped back out of sight again, going down-canyon.

I waited a moment more to see if a second rider would appear. None did. I also saw nothing more of the first rider. I quickly remounted my chestnut and gathered up the lead rope of the packhorse.

I didn't know if whoever it was had seen me, but I suspected they had. Nevertheless, I stayed out of the open as much as possible as I proceeded down the canyon. It occurred to me as I went that I should never have selected the gray for a packhorse. He was light-colored and much too easily seen against what was principally a dark background of trees.

Still, I wasn't much in a mood for caution. Maybe it wasn't Monte and Ike I had been following all this time, but I was pretty sure who had made that small boot track back there and was determined to catch up with her.

I left the canyon bottom at the base of the hill where I'd seen the rider. The climb to that small opening in the trees was steep, and it was hard to see for the trees. I guess I had my bearings pretty straight, however, for I came out almost right where I wanted to.

The clearing was even smaller than I'd thought it would be. But that was fine with me. It took just that much less time to find the tracks I was looking for. Problem was, I could only find one set when I distinctly expected to find two.

I looked around nervously. I was convinced that one of the riders I had been following all morning was the girl who rode with the mule thieves. No telling who the other one was. Had they seen me? Was I once again being decoyed?

I guess I wasn't much surprised when I heard a noise behind me. I even sort of hunched my shoulders, half expecting another swat over the head before I could turn around. But that didn't happen. I almost hated to look, but of course I did anyway.

The girl just sat there astride a wiry-looking little bay horse with a blaze face. She must have come out of the brush and trees somewhere back up the trail. She did not look to be armed, and once again she wore neither hat nor vest.

She said, "Well, we sort of thought it was you. We just weren't sure you were alone."

I looked around uneasily. "Who is 'we'?"

She gave a light smile. "Don't worry, no one's going to hit you this time. What happened to your friends?"

I peered at her. "You don't know? You weren't around last night when whoever it was shot at us?"

"I saw you from across the canyon just before it happened. You and two others and your packhorse. The gray is my horse, you know."

"Yeah," I said. "I know. And anytime you're ready I'll trade him back to you for a certain three mules and a sorrel saddle horse I happened to have lost yesterday."

She looked uncomfortable at this, but didn't say anything. In fact, she suddenly seemed to be looking right past me.

I'd just started to turn when I heard a horse nicker behind me. Then I whirled. I couldn't believe what I saw. Another girl, astride a sorrel horse, sat not fifteen yards away on the trail. Except for her hat and vest, she was the spitting image of the girl I'd just been talking to. She held a Winchester rifle across her saddle in front of her.

"Is he alone, Etta?" the newcomer asked.

"Yes, I think so."

"Okay, then, let's get out of here before Cousin Henry and the boys find us." She looked at me. "I'm hoping you know these mountains, mister. You certainly can be of help to us if you do."

CHAPTER 8

I couldn't claim to know the San Mateos like the back of my hand. But if I knew any part of them reasonably well it was the western slopes. Matter of fact, my own small homestead was probably no more than eight or ten miles in a straight line west from where I'd come upon the two girls.

At first I didn't want to go anywhere without asking some questions, about a thousand of which occurred to me at once. But the two girls seemed so absolutely anxious to get out of there I wound up leading the way posthaste on down the canyon.

What little I did learn as we went the first half mile or so was that one of the girls was named Etta and the other Ella. "Cousin Henry and the boys" undoubtedly constituted the balance of the group who had stolen my mules. They also didn't sound like very good fellows—as if I needed much confirmation of the fact—and any dealings Etta and Ella had been having with them were apparently not by choice. Seemingly, last night's shooting incident had served to create the first good opportunity they'd had to escape. This didn't explain a lot that had gone on before, however, and the more I thought about it the less I felt compelled to get myself mixed in any deeper without knowing the answer to my questions.

Beneath a couple of spreading walnut trees at the bottom of the canyon, I pulled to a sudden halt.

A girl pulled up on either side of me. From my right came "What's wrong?" It was Ella—the one with the vest and hat.

"This canyon is heading almost more south than west," I said. "Eventually it'll take us out into some pretty open country. I'm not certain that's what you want to do."

Both girls looked at me quizzically. Ella finally asked, "What do you suggest?"

"Well, I don't exactly know. Seems to me there's more to this than just getting away from Cousin Henry; more maybe I should know."

They exchanged hesitant looks. Ella said, "All we want is to get someplace they won't find us."

"And after that?"

"I . . . guess we're not really sure about that yet."

"I see," I said, intoning a definite case of the contrary.

Ella straightened in her saddle. "Look, mister . . . Lord, I don't even know your name!"

"It's O'Day," Etta interjected. "Kel O'Day. He told me so the other night." Well, at least I knew which one I'd talked to in the barn back at the cow camp, the one who had held the roundup crew at bay while her companions escaped.

"Okay, Mr. O'Day—" Ella started to say.

"Ella, he's only in this because he wants his mules back," Etta went on. "He seems like someone we can trust."

Her sister looked slightly exasperated. "You don't even know him. How can you suggest we trust him?"

"He may be someone we'll *have* to trust," came the flat response. "Who else is around to help us?"

Ella didn't have an answer.

Finally I said, "All right, look at it this way. I figure we can help one another. Like Etta says, I only want my mules back. You want something more than you've told me so far. We either trust one another or we don't. If we do, we go on from here. If we don't, I'd say we better go our separate ways right now. It's as simple as that."

Ella seemed especially uncomfortable. I looked at Etta. She shrugged. "There is a good reason for our hesitance, Mr. O'Day. Believe me, there is."

I found myself looking into a pair of gray eyes that probably could have convinced a snake it was a robin. I sighed.

"Okay. I guess I know where we can go. It'll take us a good part of the afternoon to get there, but my place is not too many miles west of here. Shouldn't be much chance of Cousin Henry stumbling onto us there."

Ella seemed relieved. "Just lead the way. We'll be right behind."

"There's only one other thing," I said. "My friends, Monte and Ike—the fellows who were with me last night. I don't know what's happened to them and my aim was to try to find them again."

Neither girl said anything, their identical expressions plainly stating they were leaving it to me to decide but hoping I wouldn't take too long in doing so.

I straightened and touched a light spur to my chestnut. "Well, they're grown men, I reckon. Surely they can take care of themselves for another day or so, if need be."

As we left the canyon, I found myself hoping someone would still be able to say the same about me when this was all over.

We entered what is called Bear Trap Canyon, a major drainage of the western slopes of the San Mateos. It is a big canyon with many feeder canyons. By May of most years, the canyon bottoms are dry, with only occasional springs, or seeps, running very low. However, the past winter had been both wet and late; springs and seeps were more active than usual and tiny clear streams still ran. Often these little trickles only remained surfaced for a hundred yards or so before going underground, but wherever we found one we expended some real effort trying to lose our trail within it.

We were riding single file down a creek bottom when one of the girls called my name.

"Mr. O'Day, could I ask a favor?" I pulled up and looked back. It was Etta.

I said, "Mr. O'Day is what folks call my pa. I'm much too young to be anything but Kel."

"Okay, then, Kel. About the favor?"

"Go ahead, shoot."

"I want to change horses."

I only stared at her.

"The gray," she said. "Remember, he's my horse. We call him Blue Boy. He's never carried a pack before, and he's a much better saddle horse than the one I'm riding."

I considered the trouble of unloading and reloading my pack, the time involved. My expression probably revealed what I thought of that request.

Ella said, "It's not worth it, Etta. Can't you just wait? That pack isn't hurting Blue Boy any."

I sort of felt that way myself, but one look at Etta was enough to convince me that I might as well get down and start unloading Blue Boy. Etta had a stubborn streak in her as plain as day.

Ella sighed and rolled her eyes skyward as I dismounted. "At least you got Blue Boy back. No telling what's happened to Little Joe."

Little Joe, I took it, was the other gray, the one Monte, Ike, and I had left back at the cow camp. I said, "I honestly don't know why I picked this horse to bring. Guess I just didn't want to take any more of the outfit's remuda than necessary. As I remember, the other gray was pretty used up. We left him in the corral at the cow camp."

"They were given to us as colts on our twelfth birthday," Etta explained, depositing her saddle nearby. "Our father found them on a horse ranch in Kansas and thought they'd be the perfect gift for us. They've been that and more, and we're very attached to them."

"Well, they sure are a match," I said, lifting the pack from Blue Boy and setting it beside the girl's saddle. "I almost could no more tell them apart than I could you two girls."

"Little Joe is a slightly lighter gray and has a white sock on his left hind foot," Ella said. "He also can run faster."

"Ha!" Etta responded instantly. "On his best day, maybe!"

After a few more minutes we had transfered packs and saddles. We left Bear Trap Canyon headed almost due west. The terrain remained mountainous and tree-covered. The canyons were deep and at or near right angles to our course of travel. Only now and then did we achieve a high point where our view was unrestricted enough to see far. When we stopped to rest our horses I looked back and was greeted with such a view.

"Pretty country, isn't it?" I remarked idly.

Etta nodded. "It makes me homesick. Especially back in that big canyon with all the fir and spruce and aspen."

"And where is home? Or is that something else I'm not supposed to know?"

"Colorado, near Kremmling—our father's ranch where we were raised. It isn't all mountains, but much of it is. Only there is more water, real rivers. I just wish we were back there . . . with our father—"

"Etta!" Ella's warning not to say more was clear and sharp.

I was about to ask more anyway, when suddenly I thought I spotted something moving on a ridge across the way. I motioned for the girls to be quiet. Whatever I had seen was no more than half a mile away.

"What is it?" Etta asked in a low voice as she tried to follow my gaze.

"Maybe nothing. Something moved over there, but I can't see it now."

We watched for another minute or so and saw nothing. The trees on the ridge were thick; whatever or whoever it was could easily remain out of sight for some while.

I told the girls, "I think we'd better go."

We eased out of sight, back among trees overlooking another canyon. The girls moaned in unison at the prospect of it.

"Don't worry," I said. "I don't think we'll have to cross this one. If we swing north a bit we should find something of a divide we can follow around the heads of several of the canyons between here and my place. When we get around there, we should be able to see a mountain I call Oak Peak. Where we're going is just west of that."

"How far?" Ella asked.

"Oh, five miles, maybe six. Why? Getting tired?"

She shrugged. "Maybe a little. Mostly just hungry. We, uh, really haven't eaten well the past day or so."

By the sun I calculated it was around 2 P.M. My own diet had been a bit slim lately, but somehow I hadn't thought twice all day about food. "I have some beef jerky wrapped inside my bedroll. Would that help?"

"Anything would help," she replied.

We chewed on jerky as we rode. The going became much faster as we struck the divide and gradually approached Oak Peak. We left the main timber behind and entered juniper- and piñon-cloaked foothills. We crossed one last canyon and topped out on a high hill where we could see forever. Dead ahead were the Luera Mountains, but a few miles away. To the northwest were the San Agustin Plains again, and thirty miles away the Datil Mountains. No more than half a mile from where we sat, just visible between two hills in a pretty little canyon, were my small cabin, corrals, and barn.

"There it is, girls. Nothing to brag about, but the house has a roof and a cookstove and you won't have to sleep on the ground tonight. The best I can offer."

"Just now," Etta said as we started off the hill, "a king's castle couldn't look any better to me."

CHAPTER 9

THE bad thing about my cabin was it had only one room. It was all one person needed but a little crowded for three, especially when two of them were young, pretty females. But it did have a covered porch. The house I grew up in had such a porch, and I'd determined so would anything I built.

We unsaddled our horses at the corrals and turned them out in the horse pasture I had spent a month fencing this past winter. I had two other horses there—the only ones I owned save for the sorrel I had lost two days before.

At the house we unloaded the pack and our bedrolls and put together a meal composed mostly of canned goods I had in my cabinets, some two-day-old biscuits from the pack, the balance of my jerky supply, and coffee.

Afterward, I caught one of the girls eyeing the bed in the far corner of the room.

"You two can share that," I said. "It's a good bed. I packed it in here all the way from Socorro. Cost me forty dollars, mostly because of the brass bedstead. It'll sure beat hard ground and a bedroll, I know that."

It was Etta who I had spoken to. "And you? Where will you be?"

"I'll be out on the porch. But don't worry, every window has wooden shutters you can latch from the inside, and the door can be bolted. You'll be safe."

"Thank you. I'm sure we'll be fine."

I strolled outside. I had a garden behind the house, which I irrigated from a spring that flowed year-round just up the canyon above the garden. It was a very dependable source but the water wasn't always the best to drink. Thus, I also had a dug well with a hand pump on it for the house. Below the corrals and inside the horse pasture was a large pond kept full by the spring's overflow.

I returned to the house a short while later with a small bucket filled with radishes and peas. I had also picked up a half-dozen eggs laid by my small flock of hens that scratched out a living down near the barn. The sun had gone behind a ridge on the west side of the canyon, and I estimated only an hour of daylight left. The girls had discovered a bathtub I kept out on the porch and had carried it inside the house. They were in the process of drawing water at the well out front and carrying it a bucketful at a time to the tub. Inside, they had started a fire in the cookstove and were heating water to take the chill out of their baths. I left the vegetables and eggs and proceeded to while away some more time outside.

It was almost dark when the girls appeared at the door, looking fresh and clean and wearing different clothes: identical plaid shirts and denim trousers, undoubtedly taken from within their bedrolls, and looking so much alike I had no idea at first which was which.

"Lord, I feel better!" one of them said. "I'm not so tired anymore."

I said, "Good. Maybe you'll feel like having our little talk now. Or are you still trying to decide if you can trust me?"

There was only a moment's hesitation before she said, "We've talked about it. We've decided."

"And?"

She sighed. "Where do you want to talk?"

We sat at the kitchen table, lamplight flickering on the walls. I had just finished helping them dump their bathwater outside. One girl sat on my left, the other across the table from me. I glanced to my left. "You're Etta."

She looked surprised. So did her sister.

I said, "I couldn't tell at first, but here in better light it's easy enough."

"Oh?" Clearly, they were unaccustomed to being so easily told apart by a stranger.

I smiled. "You went all day without a hat. Your face is sunburned. It's a dead giveaway."

I thought they looked relieved. Etta said, "I'd forgotten about that. I haven't seen a mirror in so long, no telling what I look like."

"You look just fine," I said. "But it is kind of bothersome to me that I might not be able to tell the two of you apart. Isn't there some sure way, other than clothing and sunburns and the like?"

"Well, yes, there is . . ." She seemed suddenly embarrassed and hastened to add, "But it wouldn't do you any good to know, believe me. No good at all."

Her sister laughed. "Take my word for it, what she says is true."

I took her word for it. "Okay, then. Tell me about Cousin Henry. Let's hear your story."

Etta settled a somewhat resigned gaze on me. "You must promise not to tell a soul any of this. Will you do that?"

I shrugged. "I guess if it means that much and I have a chance to get my mules back, sure. You have my word."

"All right," she said. "Cousin Henry—he calls himself our cousin—is really Henry Rutherford. He is our mother's first cousin, but she died when we were five and the truth is, my sister and I wouldn't have known Henry Rutherford from Adam until several weeks ago. With him are his two sons, Shank and Billy, who we also did not know until recently. Nonetheless, Ella and I came here with them in search of our father, Pete Ware. We came willingly, although we have been the Rutherfords' virtual prisoners ever since early in April. We don't know if our father is even alive by now, but if he is, it is very important that we find him before Cousin Henry does. It could well mean his life."

She paused for only a moment, then went on. "You see, Ella and I were born in Texas but lived briefly right here in New Mexico, in Grant County, which I understand is somewhere southwest of here. Neither of us remembers much about it because we moved to Colorado when we were three and have lived there ever since. Our mother died when we were five. I guess that's the main reason we know hardly any of her family. She was much younger than our father, only twenty-three when she died, while he was thirty-nine. Her name was Emma.

"Anyway, it wasn't easy for him after our mother died, but he doted on us so that we simply couldn't have asked for a better childhood. We loved growing up on the ranch, with our horses and cattle, and most of all, Dad.

"Then several weeks ago, Cousin Henry and his two sons showed up at the ranch. Ella and I had never seen them before, but the minute my father saw them we knew something was very, very wrong. Dad seemed to have almost no choice but to invite them into our home. Our cowboys were all away at line camps and only the three of us and an old cook were on the ranch.

"After supper that night, Henry Rutherford and our father went off together and didn't return for almost two hours. When they did come back, Dad took Ella and me aside. He told us to simply trust him. He had to make a trip to New Mexico. He would be gone no longer than a month but hopefully would be back much sooner. Shank Rutherford would be going with him, while Cousin Henry and his son Billy would remain at the ranch. He couldn't explain more, except we were to stay there too. We were to tell our cowboys and others who might come by only that the guests were our mother's kin—which, of course, was true—and would be leaving when Dad returned from New Mexico on a business trip. Next morning he and Shank saddled up and left. Just over three weeks later, Shank returned. Our father did not, and we have not seen him since."

"And you don't know what happened to him?"

It was Ella's turn to answer. "We haven't the slightest idea. We have learned why he came to New Mexico, however. Henry Rutherford finally told us the whole thing.

"You see, when Dad promised Rutherford he would return within thirty days, he apparently had no choice but to leave us as his guarantee to that. The reason goes back fifteen years, to just before our family moved from New Mexico to Colorado."

"A little of the story we knew already," Etta took over. "But most comes from what Henry Rutherford told us that night. You see, our mother's family to this day are almost all in Texas. Our father came from Missouri after the war to become a cattle drover along the old Chisum Trail. According to Rutherford, his real name is not even Ware, although you will soon understand why he changed it.

"As you might expect, Dad met our mother in Texas and married her there. Times weren't easy and they didn't have very much. All too soon twin daughters came along and that meant only that many more mouths to feed. It was Cousin Henry who first heard of better things to be had in New Mexico, a mining boom near a fast-growing place called Silver City. He also had a young family, and it was he who talked our father into making the move. They—we—all came together, it seems. Trouble was, Silver City wasn't so easy. There were constant Indian problems, and work for modest pay in the mines was the main thing to be had. It was also a hard town for women and children, and it wasn't long till both men were thinking they would be happier elsewhere. Our father apparently wanted to go north, Montana or Wyoming, where he could ranch; Cousin Henry had designs on California. But with young families to feed, it just seemed they needed a decent stake to get them started. At least, that was the rationale Cousin Henry used to talk our father into helping him and two other men hold up a mine payroll shipment."

She paused and looked at her sister. Ella said, "Things didn't work out very well. Oh, they planned it carefully, according to Cousin Henry. Even to the point of moving their families—who never knew the real reason—beforehand: The Rutherfords to Tucson, my mother and us girls to Santa Fe."

"So, what happened?"

"They pulled off the robbery one day, about ten miles southwest of Silver City. Only thing was, they were chased and cornered soon after by a posse of miners. Our father's and Cousin Henry's two partners were killed, Cousin Henry was wounded and captured, and Dad escaped—perhaps unfortunately for him—with a packhorse carrying the entire payroll. Cousin Henry was sent to prison."

I wagged my head. "Well, I've heard of stories like that. I bet Cousin Henry sat out his prison term without once spilling the beans on Pete Ware—or whatever his real name is—all the while figuring to someday get out and look your father up for his share of the haul."

"Twelve years," Etta said. "And he claims to have spent almost every day of the three years he's been out, first relocating his family, then looking for Dad. He said he never would have dreamed what actually happened to the money."

"Which was?"

"Apparently Dad was a poor thief. He told Cousin Henry that both bad conscience and fear he'd be caught with that payroll got to him almost immediately after he escaped. He made his way north through these very mountains, and on the way he stashed the payroll in a dark little canyon with a cave in it, near what he termed a 'hidden spring.' He then went on to Santa Fe, picked up his family, and proceeded north."

"And he never came back for it till now?"

"Not according to what he told Cousin Henry. He acquired his ranch strictly through honest means, by homesteading and building his own small herd into a larger one. He never again touched a penny of that mine payroll."

"And you two girls are Cousin Henry's leverage over your father, in case he and the money can be found."

"That's Henry Rutherford's view of it," she said. "But I know Dad's only motive was to return the money quietly in a way we would never know about—give Cousin Henry the whole amount—just to have it out of his life forever. I am convinced something happened to him to make it impossible for him to come back."

"Why did Shank come back without your father? Did he say what had happened?"

"Not exactly," replied Ella. "He just showed up one day on a played-out horse, and said, 'I lost him, Pa. We made it there, to those mountains he talked about. He couldn't find his bearings right off and while we were lookin' we got separated. Then I got caught in a snowstorm and I never could find him again.'"

"Cousin Henry was irate," Etta said. "He insisted Dad had pulled one over on him. We pleaded with him, told him Dad would never abandon us. Something must have happened to him."

"After three extra days," Ella continued, "when he still didn't show, Cousin Henry came to us one evening and said, 'I've decided to tell you girls about your pa. I gave him my word I wouldn't so long as he kept his and came back. He hasn't and now we've gotta go lookin' for him. Time's come you knew, 'cause you'll be goin' with us.'"

Everything was starting to make sense to me. I thought I knew which snowstorm had separated Pete Ware and Shank and I hoped my telling the girls would somehow make them feel better ".... it was a big one last month, especially up high. That's the reason there is so much live water in the canyons now. If you look just right, you can still see snow patches on the highest peaks."

A worried look crossed both girls' faces.

"And so all this," I said, "is what led to the theft of my mules and the ransacking of that cow camp," I marveled.

"They couldn't even think far enough ahead to carry provisions for themselves when they left Colorado?"

"Oh, they thought about it, to a point," Ella answered. "We left the ranch with a packhorse and a two weeks' worth of supplies. But the packhorse took sick and died before we reached Socorro. And the supplies we could carry on our saddles were all but gone a day later. I guess Cousin Henry didn't have much money. And they got to thinking about hauling out the mine payroll and the need for more provisions after the packhorse went down. Wasn't long afterward we spotted you and your mules at Magdalena. The Rutherfords just figured all along there would be a ranch someplace where they could 'borrow' anything else they needed, which is exactly what they did."

Etta straightened. "Now do you see why we asked that you not tell anyone about this? Why we can't go to the law? We just can't risk that our father might go to prison for what he did. We don't know if he's even alive by now, but if he is, it's very important that we find him before Cousin Henry does. It could mean his life."

I drummed my fingers on the table thoughtfully. "Well, I guess I don't know the law on such matters any better than you do. I do know I still want my mules back, which means finding Cousin Henry and no telling what after that. You want your dad back safe, or at least to find out what's happened to him, which probably means avoiding Cousin Henry all you can. Either way, we'll have to keep a sharp eye out every minute. And there are dark canyons with springs in them all through these mountains. No telling which one your father talked about."

"We didn't expect it to be easy," Etta said simply.

"Yeah, I know," I said. "But what I'm trying to say is, there are men in this country who know these mountains much better than I do. Are you sure you won't let me rustle up some more help?"

"Men like your two friends, Monte and Ike?" Etta asked.

"Well, yes, just like them—if we could only find them."

They both looked thoughtful. Ella said, "I just don't know. I really don't."

"Okay, just let me ask you one more thing," I said. "I accept the fact that you were these fellows' prisoners. But you also helped them. One of you distracted me when they stole my mules. And Etta, at the cow camp, you held off that roundup crew with a rifle while the others escaped. Why did you do that? I know I asked you that once before, but you never gave me an answer then."

Etta shrugged. "They had the upper hand on us, is all. If one of us tried to refuse to do something, they would threaten to hurt the other one. Too, our only hope of finding our father seemed to lay in the Rutherfords. As you said yourself, once they got to the San Mateos, Shank was the only one with even the remotest idea where Dad had gone. In some ways we needed them even more than they needed us."

"Even to the point you would shoot at those cowboys to protect the Rutherfords."

"I wasn't doing it to protect them. Remember, they had Ella. I guess I just didn't know what else to do. And I did *not* shoot at anybody. Every shot was yards high. I only meant to hold them off."

"But you finally did find a way to escape from the Rutherfords. How was that?"

Ella responded to this. "When Cousin Henry, Shank, and I went back for Etta at the cow camp that night, we left Billy in the mountains with your mules. No one figured we would have problems going back to him. But in the dark hours of morning, we couldn't retrace our trail. That's why you were able to catch up to us the next day. When we finally found Billy, it was discovered that one of the mules had gotten away. Cousin Henry and Shank went back looking for it, leaving Billy to watch us."

"We knew it might be the best chance we would get for

both of us to get away," Etta said. "Ella distracted Billy while I sneaked up behind him and got his gun. We left him tied to a tree and were making our getaway when we spotted you and your two friends just before Cousin Henry and Shank started shooting at you."

I wagged my head. "Well, that's some story. And I figure we're probably all too tired to decide anything more tonight. Maybe we should just sleep on it. There are two lamps and a lantern in here. Mind if I take the lantern with me to the porch?"

A while later, I lay awake on the porch even after the lamps were put out inside, listening to night noises and thinking. I tried to recall if I'd ever been in a canyon such as the one the girls had described. No such memory came.

I heard a noise much like something moving through the brush on a nearby hillside and wondered what it was. Presently I reached over and pulled my rifle closer to me. Any number of times I'd thought of acquiring a couple of dogs to keep around the place, the type that would bark like crazy and raise all kinds of Cain in the event of intruders. I fell asleep thinking this sure would have been a better thing to have done than just think about.

CHAPTER 10

I must have been pretty tired; I slept like a hibernating bear till the first light brightened the eastern sky. That was my normal time for waking, so I didn't think anything strange about it as I shook loose from my bedroll and felt around for my boots.

The house inside was silent, so I figured the girls were still asleep. It seemed reasonable to give them a while longer. They'd had a hard day yesterday and could probably use the extra rest. I decided I'd wander down to the corrals and see if any of the horses were in. If any were, I thought I'd keep at least one corraled in the event we needed to catch the others later.

I stopped off at the barn and got a bucket of grain, just in case a little coaxing was needed. Sure enough, two of the five horses were found watering at the pond outside the corral. The other three—as chance would have it, those we had ridden in on yesterday—had probably gone on out and were nowhere to be seen. I rattled the bucket a bit and soon had the two by the pond inside the corral. I fed them—a muscular strawberry roan and a lanky sorrel I had purchased from a neighbor six months back—at a trough on one side of the corral and closed the gate behind them.

I was on the way back inside the barn with the bucket when I noticed a light at the house. At least one window had been unshuttered and a lamp lit. Seconds later, the front door opened and one of the girls stepped gingerly down from the porch and turned the corner in the direction of the privy. I returned the bucket to its place inside the still-darkened barn, then started to step back outside. A rustling noise from somewhere inside caused me to turn back.

Only the dimmest of shapes greeted me. I had been forced to feel my way around to find the bucket and grain barrel a few minutes earlier, and it had been no better when I returned the bucket just now. Whatever it was could not readily be seen.

For a moment I just stood there. The noise could have been caused by any number of things, most of them harmless. Somehow, however, in those brief few seconds I stood motionless in the doorway, it occurred to me I should never have left the house unarmed. A voice confirmed this suspicion soon enough.

"Don't move," it rasped. "Don't even breathe deep." A gun hammer clicked back.

I didn't move. "Who are you? What do you want?"

"Never mind that. Turn around—face away from me. Don't gawk, just do it!"

Only someone who has been hit hard over the back of the head twice in three days knows how much I hated to turn my back on that guy then.

"Do it!"

I turned. A heightened pink-orange tint claimed the skyline beyond the house; two riders emerged from the morning shadows and pulled up alongside the front porch. They dismounted quickly and went inside. They were met by a startled little shriek, quickly muffled by their own gruff voices. I felt my muscles tense.

Footsteps crunched behind me. "Don't even think about it. One step and I'll blow your back open."

"Just don't hit me over the head," I told him.

"Didn't plan to," he said. " My brother's the one who did that anyway. Cross your hands behind you."

I did as I was told. He slipped a lariat loop over my wrists and pulled it tight enough to hurt. He made two more loops, yanked them tight, then said, "Okay, back inside the barn. Go slow; don't look back."

He stayed behind me as I turned. I caught a glimpse of him, but not a good one. He marched me back through the darkness to a horse stall where he backed me against a post.

"Sit down," he ordered. "Right here, on the floor."

I had to face him to do as he said. Even very close by his shape was dim, his features impossible to make out. I was helpless to do anything with my hands tied. He knelt and tied me to the post with several wraps of the rope around my shoulders and chest. Then he rose.

"Take my advice, mister. Keep clear of this deal. Them mules of yours ain't worth it. Just keep clear."

He went across to where we had deposited our saddles yesterday, rummaged around there briefly, then turned toward the door. As he went outside, his back silhouetted against the light there, I could see he was carrying a saddle with him.

I sat completely still for maybe a minute more, mostly stunned by what had happened. I couldn't see the house from my position, but I heard voices, sometimes loud, but rarely enough to be understood. This went on for a good half hour while I struggled vigorously to loosen my bonds. My wrists were rubbed raw and my hands numb by the time I heard shod hoofs striking rocks as several horses were apparently ridden away. I sat helpless to do anything as the sounds quickly died away outside.

That guy could have given lessons in tying knots. I tried everything I could think of. Nothing worked. I even tried working my way up the post to a standing position. The rope was simply drawn too tight.

Broad daylight penetrated the open doorway. I began to worry that my arms would fall off. My shoulders ached; my hands felt like lead. I had to get loose . . . but how?

Then something like a very soft footfall sounded outside. A slender form ducked through the door, stepped to one side, and hugged the wall. I heaved a huge sigh of relief.

"Hey," I said. "I'm over here."

"Mr. O'Day—Kel? Is that you?"

"Yeah, it's me. Which one are you?"

She moved toward me. "Etta. They took Ella. . . . Oh, my goodness!"

She knelt down to untie me. It wasn't easy, even for her. "I'd gone out back . . . to the privy," she explained. "I saw them ride up just as I came out. They didn't seem to see me, so I hid in some brush on the hill behind the house. They looked and looked but they couldn't find me. They finally took Ella and one of your horses . . ."

"And you just watched them go?"

"I didn't know what to do. I wanted to run right down and help my sister, but I knew I had no way of stopping them and it just seemed better they didn't get both of us. I had no idea what happened to you, only that I saw Shank Rutherford come out of the barn with a saddle. This seemed a good place to check, so I came here."

She finally got me loose. I rubbed my arms with wooden hands. "Well, you took long enough coming. I might have been dead."

She rose. "I know. But if that was true, I couldn't have done much about it, could I? And I was afraid to show myself till I was sure they were gone. I wouldn't put it past them to have stopped on a hill and waited for me to come out."

I struggled to my feet, chagrined. "I guess I'm lucky you were around at all. I just keep getting slipped up on from behind. No telling how I'd ever have got loose."

She smiled sympathetically. "Well, at least no one hit you over the head this time. He didn't, did he?"

"No—but he could have easy enough. I wasn't even smart enough to carry my rifle with me from the house. I never even got a good look at him."

"He waited for you in the barn?"

I nodded. "I figure he snuck in here while I was feeding the horses. They probably saw me leave the house and reckoned it was a good chance to waylay me without alarming you girls."

"I wonder why they didn't see me leave the house?"

"Who knows? Maybe the rest of them were up in the trees somewhere and just didn't see. You were lucky, that's all."

She didn't look very happy about it. "Well, I don't feel lucky that they got my sister. I thought you said they wouldn't find us here."

"I doubted they would," I said, "But you remember yesterday when I thought I saw something move on the hillside behind us? That could have been them, or at least one of them, on our trail. Could be they just got lucky and stumbled onto our tracks. Could be they waited till this morning—for dawn when we'd be least watchful—as the best time to come and get us."

"I guess that wasn't bad thinking, was it?" she said.

"No," I admitted ruefully. "It wasn't bad at all—thanks to me."

Again she looked sympathetic. "Well, no use placing blame now. The question is, What do we do about it? How do we get Ella back?"

"I wish I knew," I said. "The easy thing to say would be to jump on our horses and go charging off after them."

"And why not do that?"

"It might be just what they'd expect."

She stared at me. "A trap? You think they might ambush us?"

"I think they gave up looking for you awfully fast. It might be they decided the easiest way was just to take your sister and let your natural urge to go after her take care of flushing you from cover. You were probably right not to show yourself right away after they rode off."

She looked worried. "So what *do* we do? We can't just stay

here. At least I can't. Maybe you've had a bellyful of all this by now..."

"I never said anything like that. I think we agreed to help each other. I've no intention of going back on that now."

She seemed grateful, but not satisfied. "What I'm saying is, I won't hold you to that. This could get dangerous from here on out."

"It could," I agreed. "But those Rutherfords are more than just a minor irritation to me just now. And it's not just the mules. I brought you here where I thought you'd be safe. Those fellows came in here, stuck a gun in my ribs, tied me up, and took your sister. Apparently they even took one of the two horses I had left. If anybody's going after them, you can bet I am!"

She smiled thinly. "Then, we are going after them?"

"Of course, we are. We just have to be careful about it, is all. I say we go on up to the house, get some breakfast, put our gear together, and then see how quick we can catch our horses. I make no conditions on my involvement except for one thing."

Her eyes narrowed. "And what's that?"

"We could use all the help we can get in this. If we stumble across Monte and Ike, I want to be able to tell them what's going on; I'll want their help. Will you say yes to that, if the time comes?"

For a long moment she looked at me. "I know those men are your friends. But would you trust them fully?"

"With my wife, if I had one."

"Then, yes. I guess I would trust them too. If we should find them."

We stood on the porch at the house, surveying the situation. Among other things, they had taken my rifle. "They don't miss a bet, do they?" I said dejectedly.

"Are you sure they took it?"

"It was right by my bedroll. It's gone."

"Was it your only gun?"

"No, I have a six-gun I usually carry in my bedroll. I took it inside last night. Maybe they didn't find that."

They had. I had left it on a washstand in one corner of the room. There was no sign of it anywhere.

I said, "If this keeps up, won't be long till that bunch has taken everything I own. I've lost three mules, two horses, and now my only two guns."

"I had a rifle," Etta commented meaningfully. "I lost it at the cow camp."

I stared at her. "Well, I don't know if that makes us even, but it sure puts us in the same kettle of stew."

"Bad, huh?"

I didn't even bother to answer.

"So, what do we do?"

I thought about it. "Well, I can make sourdough pancakes with the batter I mixed last night. And we have fresh eggs and coffee. Maybe we'll feel more optimistic after we eat."

She sighed. "And then?"

"Everything I said before, except we go unarmed."

"And if we find the Rutherfords and Ella?"

I shrugged. "We'll shake a stick at them till they give up. And if that doesn't work, we'll think of something else. I don't know what else to say."

An hour and a half later we were down at the barn saddling two horses. Those previously missing had come in to water and were not difficult to catch. The Rutherfords had taken my sorrel, so I saddled the roan. Etta insisted she ride her gray despite my objections that it would be too easily spotted by our quarry.

"He's not *that* light-colored," she said. "And he's a much better horse than the one I rode yesterday."

We tied on our bedrolls and rode out following tracks that were already several hours old.

CHAPTER 11

THE tracks led straight east with no sign of a halt having been made. We pulled up on a high ridge about noon to study the terrain ahead. Caution had caused us to go slow.

"See anything?" I asked as Etta peered at the hillside across the canyon. She still did not have a hat, although I had offered her an old one of mine. She had declined the use of it because it was too large. As the next best thing, she had wrapped a bandanna around her head in a fashion that made her resemble an Apache Indian, albeit a very pretty one.

"Nothing," she said. "Do you?"

I hated to admit I had been looking mostly at her and hardly at all at the hillside. "No, not yet."

"They could be holed up in the trees just about anywhere over there," she said. "We might look for hours and never see them."

"Yeah, I know."

"So? What do you think?"

"I don't think they're over there."

I felt her stare. "Oh?"

My eyes were locked on a certain spot about halfway down from the crest of the ridge. "Look right over there—at that open area in the trees. Do you see?"

"I see an opening. I don't know what else you want me to see."

"Beneath that big juniper along the left ledge of the clearing. Two deer. One of them is partly in the shadow, the other not."

Finally she nodded. "Okay, I see them. They look awfully calm, don't they?"

"That's the point. I figure they're pretty much in line with the way the Rutherfords' tracks are headed. And they look settled down, like they've been there for a while. If anybody's on that ridge slope, I figure those deer sure don't know it."

"And how likely would it be for them not to know?"

"Not very. Not with three riders, their horses, and three mules to keep quiet."

"So we go ahead?"

"I'm thinking we do, yes."

"You don't think the Rutherfords are going to lay in wait for us?"

"Well, I'm not convinced of that yet. But something's sure strange about the whole thing. The way they gave up so quick looking for you; the way they struck out and so far never seem to have slowed down or looked back. I'm beginning to think they aren't much worried about what we do."

She looked thoughtful.

"Think about it. They figure we're unarmed, and they've got Ella. As long as they've got one of you, why would they really need the other one?"

"But surely they know we'll try to get Ella back."

"Like I said, they took my rifle and six-gun. What can we do? And Shank, before he left the barn, warned me to stay clear. Maybe he actually thinks I'll do that. Certainly they wouldn't be much afraid of you alone."

"It keeps coming back to the same question, then. What *are* we going to do?"

My eyes were still on the two deer across the way. "We're going to find them and we're going to get Ella back. That's what we're going to do."

It was midafternoon. We were in the bottom of a narrow canyon with towering spruce and thickets of aspen. We had stopped to have a bite to eat and rest our horses. We sat in the shade, a tiny trickle of water running before us. Horse and mule tracks crossed the creek only a short distance below where we sat.

"Are we any closer to them now than we were when we started?" Etta asked.

"Doesn't seem like it," I said. "But then, I'm not known as much of a tracker. Hard to tell an hour's difference even in droppings, much less tracks."

We had found only one place where they had stopped, probably to do the same thing we were now doing—rest and eat.

"How much daylight do we have left?"

I glanced skyward. "I guess three and a half hours, maybe four."

"What if we don't catch up to them by then?"

I shrugged. "If it gets dark, we'll just have to find a place to camp for the night and try again tomorrow. Not much else we can do."

She had an uneasy look on her face, and I decided I knew why.

"Look, if you're worried about spending the night out here alone with me—"

Her eyes shot up to meet mine. "Oh, no! It's not . . . I mean . . ."

I said, "Hey—don't worry. My mother raised me to respect women. You're in no danger from me."

She seemed contrite. "I honestly am sorry. I didn't mean to seem distrustful. It was just . . . well, I simply didn't think."

"Forget it," I said. "You don't have to apologize for something like that. I think I'd be disappointed if you felt any other way."

She seemed surprised and pleased at this.

Her eyes were what always seemed to get to me the most. I don't know if I ever saw such strikingly pretty eyes. I was beginning to feel somewhat less trustworthy than I had just represented myself.

I rose and said, "Our trail's getting cold. Are you ready?"

We found ourselves back in Bear Trap Canyon, the tracks following the canyon floor climbing.

"Where on earth are they going?" Etta asked.

"No telling. Maybe even they don't know. You were with them. Don't you have any guesses?"

"Well, they did talk several times about finding a place Shank would recognize and starting from there. Of course that was before we ever got here. Before all this confusion."

I laughed. "I bet nobody counted on someone like me taking a hand in a game such as this."

"No," she said. "They didn't. I can pretty well assure you of that."

One thing about the trail was that following it was like following a herd. Four shod horses and three unshod mules. A blind man couldn't have lost such a trail. A less-than-alert farm boy from Kansas could, however, fail to notice the sudden absence of one set of horse tracks.

Fortunately, a Colorado ranch girl was more alert. We were just past the mouth of a small feeder canyon when Etta pulled to a halt.

"Someone pulled away," she said. "I'm sure they did."

I gave her a quizzical look.

"Count the tracks."

I did. "Well, I'll be damned. Wonder when that happened."

"I don't know. I only just now noticed. We'll have to backtrack to find out."

Something I did know was our own tracks added to all the others would represent our greatest difficulty in figuring out what had happened. We rode well to the side of the original trail, back to a point about even with the mouth of the side canyon.

"Over there," I said. I had spotted a single shod hoofprint breaking away from the others in a wet spot along the creek bank. A deposit of rocks and trash where the side canyon had run water after a summer flood hid any subsequent tracks. "He went that way on purpose to keep us from noticing."

We rode a short distance above the rock pile before finding another hoofprint. Then several. We followed a single set of prints up the side canyon for maybe a hundred yards.

I pulled up. "I don't like this."

Etta looked puzzled. "What do you suppose is going on?"

"Monkey business. Has to be."

"For our benefit, you think?"

I nodded. "I don't know exactly what's what, but this is the first sign of them doing anything other than forging straight ahead."

"And?"

I looked up the canyon, searching hillsides thick with timber. "He could be up there somewhere watching to see if we come along. He might figure to spot us, then let us go on by, and tag along behind just far enough back we wouldn't see him. Could make it hard for us to get away if someone sets out to ambush us from up ahead."

"No chance it could be Ella? No chance she could have got away?"

I gave her a look. "You don't really think that, do you?"

She managed to look disappointed anyway. "No. No, I guess not. The Rutherfords wouldn't be that dumb."

I was still searching the hillside.

After a moment, Etta asked. "Well, what are we going to do? What if you're right? What if he is up there watching us?"

"If he is, he's already seen us. He should also know we've spotted his tracks. My guess is he won't know we've figured his game out, though."

"He might if you keep staring up there. He might even think you've spotted him."

Well, she was right about that. I reined around. "Try to look confused. Look all around like we've lost the tracks. We're going back to the original trail."

She did as she was told. We turned back up Bear Trap Canyon and soon left the side canyon behind. When we had gone about two hundred yards we stopped within a grove of trees.

I said, "If he's up there, I don't think he can see us now."

"What are we going to do?"

"We're going to follow those other tracks till we can find a good place to leave the trail. We'll make our tracks right with the others so he's just as likely to miss our leaving as we were his."

"And then?"

"I'm not sure, except we're going to make certain he's not behind us. If this is a trap, I damn sure don't want to fall into it."

We followed three sets of horse tracks and three sets of mule prints for almost a quarter of a mile. Then we came to another side canyon, very narrow and making a sharp bend away from us only a short distance up its length. A tiny stream joined Bear Trap Canyon at the side canyon's mouth.

"Follow me," I said as I reined my horse into the creek. We stayed in the water until we were completely beyond sight of the main canyon. A rock bluff formed one side of the canyon; the bluff overlooked a grassy clearing surrounded by trees on three sides. I told Etta, "If this isn't made to order, nothing ever will be. Let's get down and tie our horses."

She did as she was told, but asked, "Why? What are we going to do now?"

"We're going to go back on foot, find a spot where we can't be seen from the main trail, and wait. If I'm right, I figure someone'll be along shortly."

We crawled out on a low ridge that extended below the rock bluff. A thick stand of mixed brush surrounded us. At the point of the ridge we came to a spot overlooking both Bear Trap Canyon and the mouth of the side canyon.

I told Etta, "As long as we stay low, I don't think we can be seen from down there. Just get comfortable and keep your voice down."

We settled in beneath a shady pine to wait. For nearly ten minutes nothing happened.

"How long will we stay here?" Etta asked in little more than a whisper.

I knew why she was asking. The afternoon shadows were already long and the sun was almost in our eyes. I replied, "Give it a little while longer. Like I said, I sure don't want anybody behind us in that canyon."

"And if it gets dark, we wait till tomorrow and pick up the trail again?"

I nodded. "It's all we can do. We have to be patient. We have to give something a good chance to happen and be sure something bad doesn't get us first."

For a moment she just looked at me. "You know, I'm almost glad we stole your mules. At least for my sake. No telling what I would be doing right now without you."

"Well, just don't be too grateful too quick," I warned. "I may turn this thing into a real disaster before it's over."

Her eyes never wavered. "You know, somehow I just don't think that will be the case. I don't think you're the kind to let that happen."

"I wish I had your confidence," I said. "I—"

A sound from somewhere down the big canyon caused me to cut my sentence short. We both turned to look. The unmistakable clip-clop of hooves came to us just before a lone rider suddenly emerged coming round a bend. He was on a bay horse, coming at a dog trot. He seemed mostly to be watching the ground immediately ahead and alongside of him.

"That's Billy Rutherford," Etta whispered.

"Are you sure?"

"Of course. He's the only one who wears a dirty gray felt hat like that. And he's clean shaven. Both Cousin Henry and Shank are bearded."

I was watching to see if he went past the place where we had left the trail. At first I thought he would. In fact, he did—for about two paces. Then he pulled up sharply.

I said, "Uh-oh!"

He backed his horse several steps, then dismounted, kneeling to study the ground.

"I don't like this," I said. "He's seen something."

He rose, looking directly up the small creek we had traveled only a short while earlier. Suddenly he turned to his horse and swung astride. I didn't even have to see what he did next.

"Come on," I whispered. "We've got to get back to our horses before he does! Don't make noise!"

I took her hand, helping her up. I would have let go the minute she was on her feet, but she wouldn't let me. She probably didn't even realize she was doing it, but she had such a tight hold on my hand I couldn't have gotten loose if I'd wanted to.

I led the way back up the ridge as quietly as possible, then downhill toward the grassy clearing where we had left the horses. As we scrambled down the slope, I looked on up the side canyon. I wasn't encouraged by the steep inclines and bluffs I saw. The possibility loomed that we were in a box canyon with no sure way out except the way we had come in.

The horses were tied where we had left them, quietly swishing flies and little disturbed by our approach.

"Mount up," I told Etta. "Hurry!"

"What are we going to do?" She swung astride in a single fluid motion.

"We've got to beat young Mr. Rutherford around the bend right there. We've got to see him before he sees us."

Her expression was one of disbelief. "But that's precisely the way he'll be coming! We'll run right into him!"

"I know" was all I said before putting the spur to my roan gelding. There was precious little for Etta to do but follow suit.

I don't know if he heard us coming or not, but as we came pounding around that bend he sure had eyes the size of half-dollars and a mouth wide open. I don't believe he could have been more startled. For a split second he just sat there in the middle of that little creek staring at us. Then his horse shied and reared and Billy suddenly had all he could do just to hang on. It was an opportunity I hadn't expected, and I didn't pass it up.

I came even with him just as his horse landed back on all four feet and bolted up out of the creek. By chance the animal then squared to face mine. As my roan swerved to pass, I reached out and grabbed Billy Rutherford by the sleeve. It was all I could do to hang on, and because I was successful, we were both yanked from our saddles. I landed hard on my side and was unable to break my fall. I felt the wind go out of me and for several moments struggled to get my breath. Nevertheless, I was half on my feet by the time I noticed Billy Rutherford on his hands and knees, gasping with the apparent same affliction as mine.

For an instant we just stared at each other. Then he must have summoned both energy and air from somewhere, for he lunged at me. I guess he didn't even remember he had a gun holstered on his hip. He just lunged. He caught me in the chest with a shoulder and I went over backward with him on top of me. I never even knew when Etta dismounted and came running over to us. We were still rolling around on the ground, each trying to get some advantage that would enable him to swing a punch, when I heard her voice.

"Get off him, Billy! Get off him right now!"

As it turned out, he happened to be on top at the moment. I felt his muscles relax. He was astraddle my chest, his knees on the ground. He straightened and looked around with a startled look on his face. Something then reminded him of his side arm, for he slapped at his hip only to find an empty holster there.

I finally caught sight of Etta. She was standing about ten feet away, holding a six-gun with both hands, its barrel trained on Billy Rutherford's back.

"Do something stupid, Billy," she said. "Do it and I'll make a clear view where your neck used to be."

He turned just enough to see that she had his gun. He froze.

"Very slowly now. Get off him."

He got to his feet. I rolled away and did the same. We all stood there for a bit and just stared at one another.

"Well," I finally said, "at least now we have a gun."

"And Billy," Etta added. "We have Billy—one of them, just like they have Ella."

Now there was a thought: a hostage of our own! Darned me, if I didn't feel a smile coming on.

CHAPTER 12

BILLY Rutherford was about my height, with a slight build, dark hair, brown eyes, and maybe a bit hawk-faced. He also looked dusty and unkempt, but considering our recent wrestling match and his many days on the trail now, I suppose that was understandable. I certainly wouldn't have called him clean-shaven, although he probably sported only about a five-day beard. I rubbed my own bristly jaw and decided I was in a poor position to say anything about that.

Etta held the gun on him while I caught the horses. She asked as I tied them nearby, "What do we do with him?"

"I dunno. He's sure a sad-looking case, isn't he?" He looked dejected, is what he looked.

He said, "Do whatever you want. My pa's gonna kill me now soon as he finds out. Not much you could do worse than that."

Etta handed me the gun. I looked at Billy and motioned to a nearby log. "Sit down. Maybe we'll talk a bit first."

Etta seemed nervous. "It's almost sundown, Kel. Do we have time to just sit and talk?"

"That may be *all* we have time for now, other than finding a place to camp."

Billy looked even more dejected sitting on that log than he had standing. He said, "I don't have to talk to you. You can't make me."

I ignored this. "You were planning some kind of trap for us, is that right? Your pa, your brother, and you."

Silence. He wouldn't even look at me.

"You're horse thieves and kidnappers, among other things.

Not a good reputation to have in this part of the country. Bad for sure if you're turned over to the law."

Billy raised his eyes. "What law? Where?"

"There's a sheriff in Socorro. I reckon he'll do, if it comes to that."

"Bring him on" came the surly reply. "Go ahead. Just bring him on."

"You're a real kicker, aren't you? What are you, nineteen, twenty? Tough nut, right?"

Again, silence. I looked at Etta. "Well, a waste is a waste. And talking to him sure is that. I figure we better start thinking about a place to camp."

She looked around. "Not here, surely. I mean, what if Cousin Henry and Shank come back looking for Billy?"

"Yeah, I know. I've thought about that already. That's why I'm thinking here, or close to here, might not be too bad."

Etta looked at me as if she were sure she hadn't heard right. I said, "Look, we've got to come in contact with them sometime in order to get Ella back. Either we find them or they find us. I'm not sure what difference it makes as long as we know it's about to happen before they do. Now that we have Billy to bargain with, I'd say the sooner the better."

She nodded thoughtfully. "Okay, so where do you suggest? Right here?"

"No," I said. "No, I was thinking of that side canyon back there, that grassy clearing beneath the rock bluff. I think that might be the place."

"But isn't that a box canyon? Couldn't we be trapped there?"

I smiled. "We could be. But we also could set a trap there." I glanced at Billy Rutherford.

He glowered at me. "You better watch me like a hawk, mister. I'll spoil your little game in a wink if you don't."

"You know, Billy, I just this morning had a good lesson in tying a fellow's hands behind him. I've been dying ever since to try it out on somebody, and I can't think of anyone I'd rather do that on than you."

Billy glowered some more as I went over to take my lariat rope down from my saddle.

The moon was noticeably fuller and brighter each night. Stars blinked and shone in a cloudless sky. The flickering glow of our campfire danced against the face of the rock bluff. Our horses were tied just inside a stand of thick trees that grew alongside the grassy clearing. They had grazed in the clearing for over an hour before being resaddled and readied for whatever happened. Billy Rutherford lay bound and gagged in his bedroll a dozen feet from the fire.

"I sort of feel sorry for Billy over there," Etta said. "He must be terribly uncomfortable."

We sat with our backs against a huge pine trunk. I had Billy's rifle across my lap; Etta was in possession of his six-gun, which she had laid on the ground between us.

I said, "I made him as comfortable as I could. He'll just have to tough it out."

"I don't know," she said. "It's beginning to look like he'll be there all night. I'm not sure anyone's going to show up, Kel."

We had been waiting for well over an hour already. Before that we had shared a light supper with our captive, put together from the supplies we had packed inside our bedrolls. Our half-full coffee pot still sat over the coals of the fire.

"Just give it a little more time," I said. "You may be right. Dark may have caught them trying to backtrack to see what happened. But who knows? Maybe they'll spot our fire or smell its smoke. I built it as much for that purpose as any other. Maybe it'll work."

She sighed. "Even if it does, what's to say the rest of this crazy scheme won't backfire on us?"

"Nothing," I said. "Absolutely nothing."

We sat in silence for several minutes. Then Etta said, "I'm tired. I can barely hold my eyes open."

"Make yourself comfortable," I said. "I'll watch."

She changed her position slightly, her shoulder touching mine in the barest way. Presently this didn't seem to suit her and she began to feel around for a place to lie down.

She said, "You're sure you don't mind?"

"Go ahead. I'm not sleepy. I'll wake you if anything happens."

I watched the campfire gradually die to a smoldering glow, the moon creep across the sky. No telling how late it got before the fire no longer even glowed. Etta slept soundly beside me, breathing deeply and rarely turning. Billy Rutherford must even have fallen asleep, for I could hear him snoring every now and then like an old hog happily snorting around in a cornfield.

Nothing more happened, except my back grew sore and began to ache from leaning against the pine trunk. I caught myself nodding uncontrollably. I rose quietly, so as not to wake Etta, stretched my legs and back, then went back to check the horses. They were restless, tired of standing tied in one spot. I fed them a few handfuls of grass and spent a little time simply calming them. After a while I retook my place alongside a still-sleeping Etta.

I thought of waking her so she could take over my watch the minute I started nodding again. She seemed so peaceful I hated to, so I didn't. I should have; I just didn't.

I dreamed the sun was up and someone was lifting my rifle from my lap as I slept. I opened my eyes with a start and saw I wasn't dreaming. A rifle barrel stared at me from no more than a foot away. I felt around for the six-gun Etta had laid between us last night, but it too was gone.

"I found 'em, Pa! I found 'em both right over here!"

Shank Rutherford's expression was only a hair short of gleeful. A smile split his black beard and his eyes actually sparkled. I could see Billy's six-gun stuck inside his belt. The sun just peeked over the ridge past his right shoulder.

Etta stirred nearby. She had pine needles in her hair and on her clothes as she sat up blinking.

"I warned you, buster. I told you to stay clear."

A second bearded figure was working busily over the still-prone Billy Rutherford, untying him. Nearby stood three saddled horses and my mules. Astride one of the horses—that sorrel of mine taken yesterday—sat Ella. Her hands appeared tied to her saddle horn.

Billy Rutherford got to his feet looking like an old man trying to get the cold out of his bones on a bitter winter morning. His pa strode forcefully our way, rifle in hand.

Etta looked at me in obvious dismay. "How did this happen, Kel?"

I was staring uncomfortably at the rifle barrel in my face. "All I know is, I fell asleep and woke up to this."

Henry Rutherford was almost the exact same height as his older son. However, he was heavier by maybe twenty pounds, the lines around his eyes were much more deeply etched, and his beard and the hair beneath his hat, seen close by, were streaked with gray.

"Back away, Shank," he ordered gruffly. "No need to stick that rifle barrel in anyone's mouth."

"Thanks," I said, my appreciation genuine.

He told Shank, "Go help your brother and untie Ella." He surveyed Etta and me solemnly. "Well, we sure have complicated each other's business of late, haven't we? Etta, you all right?"

She got to her feet, dusting off her clothes with her hand as she spoke, "No thanks to you, Cousin Henry. No thanks to you at all."

"Sorry you feel that way, girl. You and Ella hadn't got away the first time we mighta found your pa by now. As it is, we've wasted more'n a little bit of time and ain't found nothin' or no one."

I, too, got to my feet. "You have three mules and a horse of mine. I think you've lost more time taking other folks' property than you have doing anything else."

"Well, there's truth in that, all right. Just goes to show, no one can cover all the bets. We needed what we took though. Wouldn'ta done it otherwise."

He seemed so perfectly satisfied with this justification of his actions, I couldn't think of a thing to say to the contrary.

"What are you going to do with us?" Etta asked.

For a moment he just looked at her. "Reckon that's the main question, all right. Yes, sir, it is." Behind him, Shank had untied Ella's hands. She dismounted and came our way.

"Are you all right, Etta?" she asked. "Mr. O'Day—Kel?"

Etta said, "We're okay. You?"

Ella nodded as she came to stand beside her sister and looked expectantly at Rutherford. "I heard what my sister asked you. What *are* you going to do with us now?"

He looked around. "Well, reckon I'm not sure yet. Maybe we'll just build a fire, boil some coffee, make breakfast, and talk about it. Maybe that's what we'll do."

As we walked toward our now-dead campfire, Billy Rutherford said to his pa, "I just hope you'll let me show 'em what it's like to sleep all tied up, Pa. I sure as hell do."

The older man gave him a hard stare. "Seems to me it'll be right interestin' to find out how you got yourself into that fix in the first place, son. But that's for later. Right now, you go hunt up their horses and bring 'em here. I wanta talk a bit about how this young man might just be of some help to us in findin' what we're lookin' for. Yes, sir, I sure do!"

CHAPTER 13

WE sat around the fire, drinking coffee. It almost seemed an amicable atmosphere. One of my mules brayed from nearby. All three carried packsaddles, but only one carried a pack. They appeared to be in good shape.

Shank held a rifle on the girls and me. I wondered if he'd use it, and decided he might. Neither of the two boys seemed all that smart. If there were any brains in the family, I figured the old man or the boys' mother had them. Whether any of that had anything to do with being willing to shoot unarmed people, including females, I had no idea.

Henry Rutherford said, "Now, I'm sorry about your mules and the horse. You know all about our problem here, so you'll just have to understand. Maybe if you help us, you'll have a chance to get them back."

I was thinking about Monte and Ike, wondering again what had happened to them. Was Rutherford also sorry about taking those shots at us?

"How can I help you? I've already told the girls here I don't know of a place called Hidden Spring. I don't recognize their description of the canyon it's in."

"Shank thinks he can find his way to about where he last saw my old friend Pete. We hope to start on the right track from there. From what Pete told him at the time, the canyon we're lookin' for is still well to the south of where he and Shank got separated. He thought it was about a third of the way north from a group of high peaks on the south end of the mountain to the highest peak on the north end. The canyon drains northeast into a larger canyon and is maybe three miles long. The spring seeps from the base of a high rock bluff with wild grapevines all over its face. There is a cave all but hidden by the vines, which Pete stumbled onto by accident while tryin' to get a drink. That cave is what we're lookin' for."

I glanced at Etta and Ella, then said, "Well, that narrows it down some, at least. Those high peaks on the south number a half a dozen in the ten-thousand-foot range, or so I'm told. They also occur over an area of twenty-five or thirty square miles. It's rough country, let me tell you. The high peak on the north is probably Mount Withington, which you can see from here, east and some south of us just now. Elevations drop considerably between it and the big peaks to the south, something like a huge saddle. The canyons are steep and rough, and the going to get there will be slow. You could go forty miles on flat country before you go five or ten anywhere here."

"And the canyon?" Rutherford asked. "Anything familiar in that description?"

I shook my head. "There are canyons everywhere. I don't recall seeing one like it."

"But I reckon you have been in the part of these mountains we're talkin' about. Maybe more'n once."

"Yes," I admitted. "Yes, I have. I've hunted deer and bear in that area. But only a couple of times. I know the west side of the mountains much better than the south or east or middle."

Rutherford seemed thoughtful. "Well, the way I figure it, you know 'em all better than we do. I reckon you could help us more'n a little bit."

"And what makes you think he'd want to do that, Cousin Henry?" It was Etta, voicing my very thought. "What have you done for him, except cause him trouble?"

Rutherford laughed. "Don't reckon it matters whether he wants to or not. Case you haven't noticed, we got the drop on him, not him on us."

"You're going to make him help you?"

The man's eyes narrowed. "If it comes to that, yeah. I don't reckon he'd like the other choices we have of what to do with him. He's lucky I think he could be of some help."

"And what about us, Ella and me? What about all three of us if you find what you're looking for? What about Dad?"

He settled a hard gaze on the three of us. "You girls want your pa back, you best cooperate from here on out. Cowboy here wants his health to remain the same, he best help us. All I want is what's mine. I get it, I go my own way, and you go yours."

"Do you really consider that stolen mine payroll yours?"

"It's as much mine as anybody's. I served my time for it. I mean to have it."

"And Dad? What about him?"

"He don't want it. All I wanted from him was to help me get it back. He don't matter to me otherwise."

"But what if something's happened to him? What if we don't find him?"

"That's your worry, not mine. We'll never know anyway unless we go lookin', now will we? What I'm askin' you folks to do is climb on your horses peacefully and lead the way. Quit causin' us trouble and holdin' up the search."

The girls and I exchanged looks.

Rutherford rose abruptly and looked down on us. "I figure I'm bein' reasonable here, maybe beyond what I should be. Don't make me start thinkin' otherwise. Do you agree to do as I say or not?"

Ella said, "I don't see that we have much choice."

"Will you let us go if you find the money?" Etta asked.

"Sure, why not?" he said, although a bit evasively. He looked at me. "We'll even give any mules we don't need back to you. And your horse. Might even pay you for your trouble and anything you don't get back. What d'ya think of that?" Then he laughed, a big booming laugh, in which he was joined by his two sons. "Ain't that a fair deal, huh? Ain't it?"

Somehow, I didn't feel like giving him the pleasure of an acknowledgment. Finally I said, "Okay, if we're going to do it, then let's do it. We'll never find that fool canyon with a cave and a spring in it sitting here."

Rutherford almost beamed. "Now that's the way I expect to hear a smart young man talk. Yes, sir, that's the way!"

Fifteen minutes later we were mounted and on our way back toward Bear Trap Canyon.

Wherever the trail was wide enough, we rode in pairs: Rutherford and me, followed by the two girls, with Shank and Billy bringing up the rear and leading the mules. By this method they kept us more or less surrounded. Unarmed, we certainly weren't very likely to try to get away, but the Rutherfords seemed determined not to take any chances.

We made Monica Saddle about midmorning. There we stopped. It was a place Shank insisted he remembered from his trip to the San Mateos with Pete Ware.

"Was near here that we got separated that night," he told us. "There's a good trail on south from here that goes on past the big mountain up there." He was looking at Mount Whithington. The trail was the same one I had followed three days earlier while tracking Etta and Ella.

Henry Rutherford looked at me. "You know where that trail goes?"

"A dozen possibilities," I said. "What I know of it, there are forks everywhere. Some of them are only deer trails. Others I don't know. People come into these mountains for different reasons."

"Like?"

I shrugged. "Some come here to hunt game. Others look for stray cows. Some search for gold and silver. Fact of the matter, I've heard about a new mining camp that's sprung up somewhere on the east side since winter. I'm told they're calling it Rosedale. A fellow named Richardson is supposed to have discovered gold there last fall."

Cousin Henry looked intrigued. "You don't know where it is?"

"Not exactly. Somewhere south and east of here, I think. I understand it's somewhere near the upper reaches of what's called North Canyon. That's six or seven miles from here, straight away."

"Will we have to go past it to get where we're goin'?"

"Well, since I don't know exactly where we're going, I guess I don't know what we'll have to go past. My guess is we'll come no closer than four or five miles. I figure if we're smart, we'll stay with the crest of the mountains and not venture far down slope until we spot a canyon we're sure we want to investigate."

"What if this canyon with the hidden spring ain't very near to the crest? What if we miss it?"

"I guess there's that chance. Do whatever you like. I just figure if a man came through here fifteen years ago making his way north with the idea in mind to make the trip as fast as possible, he'd stay with the crest. Otherwise he crosses canyons constantly, no matter whether he takes the east slope or the west. I figure if he came across his hidden spring and cave that way, so should we."

Rutherford nodded slowly. "Makes sense, I reckon." He looked around. "Okay. We'll stay with the crest. And we avoid this Rosedale camp. I don't wanna be explainin' to no nosy miner what I'm about. You understand, cowboy?"

"I understand."

We took lunch about a mile south of Whithington Peak. From there we wound our way south over a trail that was often steep, generally slow, and seldom wide enough for us to ride other than single file. Midafternoon found us at a fork in the trail, debating which way to go.

Neither fork seemed to maintain a clear-cut southerly direction, but there were horse and boot tracks on the fork that went left, going and coming.

"I have a feeling that'll lead to Rosedale," I told them.

"These tracks could be miners who have been up here looking for game."

"You're sayin' take the right fork?" Rutherford asked.

"That's what I would do."

Rutherford looked at his eldest son. "Shank, you remember any of this?"

"I dunno, pa. It was already cloudy that afternoon when we got separated. I'm sure we came something like this, but I'm not sure we ever got this far."

We took the right fork. For a ways I wound up riding alongside Etta.

She spoke in low tones. "What's going to happen, Kel? Are we really going to help them find that place?"

"Maybe. If we can. Why not?"

"I don't trust him, Kel. I'm trying, but somehow I just don't."

I nodded. "Yeah, I know what you mean. I guess I don't either."

The trail narrowed, and it was back to single file. We didn't get to talk like that anymore while we were riding.

Several times we found dim trails going off into steep canyons draining east. There never were any more than bear or deer tracks on any of them. A couple of times we stopped to let Billy or Shank ride down one of these trails to see if anything about the canyon looked promising. Once, while this was going on, I happened to glance back the way we had come. Movement on a hillside almost a mile away caught my eye instantly. What I thought could be a horse and rider came momentarily into view between stands of trees. I looked around to see if anyone else had noticed. No sign was evidenced that they had. I glanced back just in time to see a second flash of movement in the same place as the first. A second horse and rider? My pulse beat faster as I considered it. Could someone be on our trail?

I didn't get a chance to repeat my looks back. Shank came riding back up the trail and announced that not only did nothing look promising down there, but he thought we must have strayed off the crest. What we had thought drained east looked more south, later turning west. As I looked at it, then at the sun behind me, I decided he was probably right.

"We'll have to backtrack to the last fork," I concluded. "Some of these ridges will fool you. Everything twists and turns so much it's hard to keep a direction."

We went back, took the other fork, and decided sundown would catch us if we did not find a place to camp soon. Below us on a broad bench was an open park overlooking a shallow canyon with tall pine and patches of gangling oak. It seemed a reasonable chance there was water in the canyon. We made our way down there in about a half hour and were not disappointed. It was an ideal place to camp—water, plenty of grass for the livestock, and shelter. The afternoon had been breezy, and getting out of the wind with night coming on appealed to us almost as much as did the water.

Etta, Shank, and I staked the horses and mules out to graze, while the others gathered wood for a supper fire and went through the pack deciding what to fix to eat. Some might call it skimpy fare, but we were hungry enough to eat almost anything. Coffee, fresh fry bread, canned fruit, and bacon weren't bad.

After supper, a discussion took place among the Rutherfords regarding what to do with the girls and me overnight.

I knew beforehand what Billy was going to say. "Tie 'em up, pa. It's the only way. Take turns watchin' 'em, too. I'll be glad to go first."

"You"ll go when I say," the father returned gruffly. "Shank?"

"Can't trust 'em, pa. Tie 'em up."

He looked at us. "They're right, you know. Reckon you'll understand."

We sat around the fire, coffee cups in hand. There wasn't any use protesting—I guess we all knew that.

It was full dark, a bright moon swimming rapidly among

fluffy clouds that raced across the sky. The wind had lessened considerably in the canyon, but could still be heard rustling leaves high up in the aspen.

They tied our hands in front of us with lariat ropes, then took the loose ends and tied our feet without slack so we could lie on our sides in our bedrolls but could do little else. Our bedrolls were located at least fifteen feet apart, thus preventing any secretive discourse between us. Rutherford himself took first watch over us.

For a while I lay awake, trying to get comfortable. The realization that this was not going to be possible came quickly. Still, I decided I had to make the best of it and get whatever rest I could. I fell asleep with the fire flickering low and one of my mules braying at God only knows what mules bray at.

CHAPTER 14

SOMEONE was whispering in my ear. I felt the tickle before I could discern the words. I came awake slowly at first, then with a start.

A soft hand settled quickly on my shoulder. "Shhh! Quiet! It's me—Etta."

I blinked, trying to see through sleepy eyes. It was still dark. The moon must already have gone down, for other than bright stars and the dim glow of a near-dead campfire off to one side, there was no light. There were snores from across the camp. I rolled partway on my back. Etta's face was within six inches of mine.

"Shhh!" she warned again. "They're all asleep. Billy is supposed to be watching, but he's been snoring for thirty minutes. They didn't tie me very well. I've already untied Ella. She's gone to catch the horses."

I still wasn't quite awake. All I could think about was the covers of my bedroll had slipped and the night air was cold.

"Here," Etta whispered. "Let me get your hands loose."

My back hurt; my legs and arms hurt; my hands were numb or I'm sure they would have hurt, too. As soon as Etta had them untied, I sat up and flexed them. Then I reached for my feet.

Etta crouched beside me as I finished loosening my bonds. "You get our saddles; I'll get the bedrolls."

I never really questioned what we were about. It seemed a little crazy, but there wasn't time to debate. I rose as quietly as possible and slowly gathered up my saddle and blankets, which lay nearby. It was impossible not to make at least some noise, but the snoring across the way never faltered. I carried my saddle with one hand and Etta's with the other, lifting them high enough so nothing would drag on the ground as I went. It wasn't easy, as I had saddle blankets trapped under each arm to boot.

About halfway to the horses I stepped on a branch. It cracked loudly and I froze. Ahead, I heard Ella whisper, "Who is it? Kel? Etta?"

"It's Kel," I whispered back, almost too loudly.

Nothing seemed to happen behind me, so I resumed making my way forward. Dim shapes took form as I approached Ella and three bridled horses. Moments later, we heard Etta's soft footfalls coming up behind me.

I said, "Start saddling. I'll go back for the other saddle."

"Be careful," Etta said. "One of them almost woke up when you stepped on that branch."

I returned for the other saddle as quietly as I could. Somehow I managed not to step on another branch. I hefted the saddle, carefully placing the cinches so they wouldn't drag. As I was feeling around for Ella's saddle blanket, a snore was interrupted by a snort and a loud smacking of lips. At the same time someone rolled over in his bedroll. For several moments I only stood there. Nothing else happened, so I turned and started a cautious retreat. It had been in my mind to try to take a rifle and perhaps some food; now I was afraid to risk it. I made my way on back to the girls and the horses.

The girls had almost finished their saddling. Etta asked, "What should we do about their horses and the mules? Turn them loose?"

I couldn't help smiling. "Sure would serve them right, wouldn't it? I hate to see my mules loose in these mountains, though. I don't know."

"Couldn't we take the mules with us?"

I had already been considering this. "Let their horses loose while I finish saddling. We'll see about the mules if we have time."

I was just buckling the flank cinch on my saddle when I

heard a commotion near where the horses had been staked. Then I heard what seemed an involuntary cry from one of the girls. Something big plunged through the grass and crashed into some nearby brush. Hoofbeats pounded. And if that wasn't enough, splitting the night air was the loud braying of one, then all three, of the mules.

Amidst all kinds of cursing and hollering from the camp behind me, I swung astride and yelled for the girls to do the same. There was no time whatsoever to be fooling with those damned mules.

Daybreak found us back atop the mountain crest. It had been slow going in the dark; slopes were steep, the trail winding, and I figured it a major accomplishment we had even managed to find the way.

The morning air was chill, and we didn't have a coat between us. Too, sometime during our escape, Ella had lost her hat and Etta had mislaid her headband. On top of all else, I was back to having problems telling them apart. About the only way was when they were mounted—Etta on the gray, Ella on the sorrel. Even that presumed they didn't for some crazy reason switch mounts on me.

We pulled up to look back the way we had come. I said, "I'm not sure this was a good idea. We have no food, no weapons. We might have been better off where we were."

"That's not quite true," Etta said. "I managed to get three tins of corned beef, a sack of fry bread, some bacon, and a skillet inside my bedroll."

I looked at the roll on the back of her saddle. It had a big lump in its middle where the skillet must be. I felt better instantly.

"Okay, that helps. Next thing is to decide where to go from here."

Both girls looked puzzled.

"You wanted to get away," I explained. "What did you have in mind to do afterward?"

Etta finally said, "Why, go on looking for the canyon with

the hidden spring, of course. It may be the only clue we ever have about what's happened to our father."

I was still looking back the way we had come. The immediate stretch of canyon below remained in morning shadow and did not offer much to see. However, from our vantage point I could see well into the distance—down past the San Mateo foothills and the south end of the Magdalena Mountains, across a broad, dissected fan that reached all the way to the Rio Grande thirty miles away.

Ella asked, "How long do you think it will take the Rutherfords to catch their horses and come after us?"

"No telling," I said truthfully.

The sun rose as we made our way uphill along a well-defined ridge. We rode among pine and oak, careful not to lose our bearings and go off to the west as we had the day before. Slopes steepened and the ridge narrowed as we went; canyons headed to both our right and left, sometimes dropping away too steeply to even consider entering them on horseback. We stopped to look back at every high point, but only briefly.

Finally on a high hill we dismounted to rest our horses and unload Etta's bedroll. We were loath to start a fire for the obvious reason, but we could at least eat some of the fry bread. The combined warmth of a sun now an hour and a half in the sky and the welcome taste of food did wonders for the way we felt.

We sat and studied the way we had come; no sign of pursuit yet. We scanned the canyons within our view for one that might invite closer inspection. We tried to imagine the girls' father having come this way fifteen years earlier, going north. How would it happen he might enter one of the canyons? Why would he want to? Looking for water, perhaps?

I found myself looking at the two girls. They sat side by side atop a jutting outcrop a dozen steps away. They looked so much alike I would never have told them apart had I not known which was which when they dismounted a short while earlier. Sometimes I sensed a difference in their personalities. I thought Etta perhaps the steadier of the two, Ella a bit unpredictable. But then, I hardly knew them. . . .

I broke their reverie as I said "See anything?"

Etta, sitting nearest me, gave a little jerk. "Oh . . . no. Do you?"

"Not yet."

Ella said, "Maybe they couldn't pick up our trail."

"Possibly. But somehow I hate to count on it. I didn't think they'd find us once before, remember?"

"We remember."

I was back to studying the canyons. "I think we're far enough south now to be in the area we're looking for. That big canyon stretching down onto the flats is probably what's called East Red Canyon. Its main tributaries come in generally from the south, draining down from the high peaks behind us. Could be one of those is the canyon with the hidden spring."

Both girls turned their gazes south. The country looked rough, elevations rising rapidly toward a number of peaks, the highest remaining several miles away straight across and no telling how far over tortuous terrain. A long canyon drained northeast between our hill and the nearest peak of significance. I could see where it most likely drained into East Red Canyon, three or four miles away. At least five discernible feeder canyons, including upstream forks, merged with the long canyon before it reached the East Red. One of those tributaries headed at the base of the hill we were on. The problem was, how to get down there? Slopes were steep and rocky; any descent into the canyon from our present location would be almost impossible.

I turned back to the girls. "Let's stay with the ridge and see if we can make our way around to the head of that canyon there. I have no idea if it's the right one or not, but it sure fits the only description we have. I'd like to check it out if we can find a way down."

We left the hill and continued following the ridge. Deer trails went here and there off the ridge, but none were inviting to horse and rider. We skirted two more hills and crossed through a narrow saddle. Descent toward the canyon bottoms still appeared impractical.

I said, "It's not likely your father would go off in a place like this; I see no reason for us to consider it. Let's go on around."

We jumped two deer as we topped the next hill. They bounded through the trees on up the ridge. We picked up their tracks as we proceeded along the trail. They followed a well-worn path that had tracks coming and going. Presently the trail forked, one side staying high on the ridge top, the other cutting back toward what appeared to be a primary fork of the canyon. Still following fresh deer tracks, we took the second fork.

I told the girls, "Deer going back and forth from a canyon like that should mean there's water down there."

The trail wound between tall trees and brush, generally keeping to the contours of the slope but at places steep and difficult. I began to think that about the only way a person would make such a descent was when he didn't realize what he was getting into when he started. Our horses struggled repeatedly to keep their footing. I was glad the ground wasn't wet and slick.

It took a good half hour to reach the bottom, which was narrow and rocky. Nothing looked very promising. We pulled up to consider whether or not to go farther. A light breeze was in our faces.

Ella was looking around curiously, her nose wrinkled. "I smell something. It's . . . it's like something dead."

Suddenly, I smelled it too; not the overwhelmingly sickening odor of something in the early stages of decomposition, but not like anything alive either.

"Etta?" I asked.

She, too, was looking around. "Yes, I smell it. But I don't see—"

I had let my horse start forward, going only a few steps farther down the trail. He approached a boulder and a deadfall of pine and was about to step past the boulder when he made an abrupt stop. Ears forward, he snorted loudly and balked at further progress. I gave him a good spur, just to get him to go far enough so I could see what it was he'd shied at. I saw what it was just as he refused once more to go on and tried to whirl away.

"Oh, hell," I said, instinctively motioning for the girls to stay back. I was too late. Etta was already at my side and Ella was right behind her.

Lying twisted and half-hidden within the trunks and branches of the deadfall was the rotting carcass of a horse. The animal lay half-rolled on its back, its head twisted tortuously as if it had died of a broken neck. It still wore a saddle and bridle and was covered with flies.

"Oh, my God!" Etta cried. "That's Dad's saddle! And I'm sure that's Jasper, his favorite horse, the one he left home on. It is, isn't it, Ella?"

Ella urged her mount closer, standing in her stirrups in order to see better. The dead animal's hide—what hadn't been eaten away by vultures and coyotes—was stretched and torn by the rotting process, but its mane and tail were more or less intact and one could at least tell it had been either a dark bay or a chestnut with a white stocking on its left hind leg.

Ella gave a worried nod of confirmation. "Yes, that could be Jasper, and I'm certain it's Dad's saddle."

I dismounted for a closer look. The animal could have been dead for a month or more. The saddle had a rifle scabbard, but this was empty. I also could find no sign of a bedroll. A lariat rope lay half-uncoiled a dozen yards away.

Neither girl dismounted. They seemed afraid of what they

might find. I looked around some more. The carcass lay at the base of a low bluff, from which the animal conceivably could have fallen. Had the horse been riderless when it happened? If not, where was the rider now? I could find no sign of a body, no clue what had happened to him.

I returned to my horse, shaking my head. "Nothing. I don't know if that horse was ridden off that bluff or what, but if it was, whoever rode him isn't here now."

Looks of immense relief greeted this statement. Etta's, however, didn't last long. "But where could he have gone? If he survived, what's happened to him?"

I looked on down-canyon. There was a bend perhaps two hundred yards away where another fork joined ours. "I dunno. But this might be the canyon with the hidden spring and it might not. He may have been just as lost as we are when he rode off into it."

Ella looked doubtful. "This is a rough little canyon. Why would he come into it if he wasn't pretty sure it was the right one?"

I shrugged. "Maybe he thought that, all right. Who knows? Remember the snowstorm? A man can get awfully disoriented in one of those."

We followed the canyon on down to the bend. Sure enough, the mouth of the other fork greeted us. It seemed no less steep and narrow than the one we were in, its rocky bottom dry. None of us saw anything prospective about it. We decided to proceed on down the main canyon, which at least did appear to widen ahead of us.

We were approaching the mouth of another side canyon, making our way along a trail that dipped in and out of an otherwise dry creek bed, when I suddenly noticed a tiny trickle of water among the rocks of the creek bottom. I pulled to a halt.

Etta stopped right behind me. "What is it?"

"A seep. Not much, but it's something."

She looked down at the small pool of water at my horse's

feet. "Hardly what you'd call a spring, is it?"

Ella was looking around. "I don't see a rock bluff or any grapevines."

"Yeah," I said. "No cave, either."

A short distance farther down the canyon the seep disappeared entirely. It was past noon; the day had grown warm but was not uncomfortable, especially in the shady bottom of the canyon. But the girls were thirsty and so was I. When one needed water, there was nothing but a putrid little seep in the rocks.

"Maybe a little farther down," I suggested. "I just can't help but believe your father was near where he wanted to go when he reached this canyon."

The canyon was dry all the way to the next side canyon. No sign of a spring, rock bluff, or cave; no sign whatsoever of a man named Pete Ware.

The girls looked tired and discouraged; increasing strain showed on their faces. Something had happened to their father's horse, and it was reasonable to believe something had happened to their father as well. But what? If he had survived the fall with the horse, where had he gone? If he had lived, why had he failed to show back up by now?

"I don't care about the spring and the cave anymore," Etta moaned. "I never cared about that stolen payroll. I just want to find Dad."

"I know," I said sympathetically. "And I have no idea what to suggest. Except maybe we should go back to the only thing we've found so far—back to the dead horse. Could be we rushed off too quickly and overlooked something that would have helped."

Neither girl looked hopeful, but finally Etta said, "Okay. Maybe you're right. But shouldn't we follow the canyon on out first? I mean, we've come this far . . ."

Of course, she was right about that. It would be a shame to quit just short of finding something.

It took less than an hour to reach the mouth of the canyon, which at that point opened out into a much larger drainage that flowed east. I was pretty sure we had reached East Red Canyon.

A midafternoon sun burned down on us now, and our thirst had not been slaked. The canyon's sandy creek bottom was wet and in places had tiny pools infested with water bugs and the like. On the assumption we might find something better upstream, we rode west for about a hundred yards. Even before we reached the spring, we came upon running water. Its source actually bubbled from beneath twin rocks of near-boulder size. We dismounted before a glassy little pool that could not have looked better if it was an icy mug of beer.

We drank our fill, then let our horses do the same. Etta was just in the process of suggesting we consider making camp and going back to the dead horse tomorrow when the loud bray of a mule caused her words to freeze in midsentence.

We had almost forgotten about our friends the Rutherfords. The mule's bray echoed down the canyon, only to be followed by a yell and a curse. For a moment we weren't even sure which way to look, but then I glanced up and saw where he was.

High on the point of a ridge above us sat a lone rider. Even if we had not heard the bray, we would have recognized his long-eared mount as a mule. Seconds later he reined around and was gone.

All I could say was "Dammit! Dammit all to hell!"

CHAPTER 15

THE best we could hope for was that the rider was alone and had to go back for his companions. Too, it might take them a while to find a way down off that point to come after us.

"Come on," I told the girls. "Mount up and follow me."

We went up-canyon at a high trot. No more than a quarter of a mile away was the mouth of a side canyon. When we got there we pulled up to study our position. The side canyon looked steep but passable. I chose not to linger. We rode up a gravelly creek bed and in among tall trees. It was something of a climb and our horses were already tired, so we slowed to a walk.

"We're out of sight and I don't think they saw which way we went," I said. "Let's just see where this takes us."

The canyon just kept climbing. It also turned out not to be very long. We entered stunted fir and aspen. Total shadows claimed our immediate surroundings as the sun went behind the ridge on our right. The canyon headed less than a mile up its length and we were forced to set out on a steeper climb yet. A seldom-used deer trail led us up a side slope toward a high ridge. Several times we stopped to let our horses regain their wind. On each occasion we looked back for signs of pursuit. As yet, there were none.

We topped out on a narrow ridge that overlooked another canyon. After a brief discussion, we decided to stay with the ridge. The climb was much more gradual now, but we knew we could only push our horses so hard. We stayed with a walk.

The sun sank rapidly as we went. We began to think in terms of nightfall and making camp. It seemed we had outdistanced our pursuers for the time being, which was a definite relief. We doubted our horses could take much more punishment without a rest.

We dropped into another canyon, a reasonably easy descent this time. A flock of turkey ran, then flew, noisily in all directions before us. We weren't surprised to find water in a canyon with turkey in it: a spring at the base of a steep slope near the head of the canyon.

We unsaddled our horses, watered them, and staked them out to graze in a small clearing adjacent to the spring. I gathered firewood while the girls untied bedrolls and broke out our small supply of food.

"Are you sure it's safe to have a fire?" Ella asked as I searched my own gear for matches.

"A small one," I said. "I think it's a worthy risk, considering the choice between something cold to eat and something hot. And you already know how cold the nights can be at this elevation. That and us with no coats."

The moon was halfway across the sky by the time full dark was on us. We dined on corned beef, bacon, and fry bread, bemoaning only that we had no coffee to go with it and that we had to eat with our fingers out of cans and a skillet. I smiled as the girls crowded closer and closer to the fire.

"What are we going to do, Kel?" Ella asked. "This all just seems so hopeless. Poor Dad . . . there's no telling what happened to him. If he's alive, he surely isn't still around here. And we have no idea where to look."

"That's just the point," I said. "Somewhere around here may be our only clue. I still think we should go back to that dead horse and start again. If we can just find that spring and the cave, maybe we'll at least learn if what he was looking for is still there."

"And if it's not?"

I could only shrug. I didn't really know.

Etta said, "I think Kel's right. Dad never came home. If he left these mountains—if he was able to leave them—he would have gotten home somehow. He couldn't have been far behind Shank."

"What about the Rutherfords?" Ella asked. "How long can we go on dodging them?"

That was bothering me, too. We had no weapons, and presented with day after day of this, there were limits on how long our horses would hold out. We had been lucky so far. No telling how long that would last.

After a bit both girls decided they needed to leave the fire and go find a bush somewhere. They disappeared in the darkness together. Minutes later one came back, then the other. They retook their positions by the fire, silently warming their hands. All of a sudden I realized I didn't know for sure which was which again. They still wore those identical plaid shirts. One way or the other, I'd kept track of them by which rode which horse, or which answered to which name. It was easy enough to precede a statement or question by saying Etta or Ella and see which one responded. Still it intrigued me how one might tell them apart otherwise.

Presently one of them said, "I'm tired. I think I'll turn in."

We all said "Good night," and two of us watched as one spread her bedroll out a dozen or so feet from the fire.

For almost a minute nothing was said. Finally I rose. "I think I'll go check the horses."

"Can I go with you?" my companion at the fire asked.

"Sure."

Moonlight brightened the clearing ahead of us. Etta's gray was the easiest to locate. The sorrel and the roan were nearby where they were supposed to be, their stake ropes tied to heavy rocks they could not pull. All seemed normal with the animals.

Nonetheless, we tarried while checking them. Presently I said "Etta?"

She turned to me, her face white and very pretty in the moonlight. "Yes?"

"Well, I guessed right, I wasn't sure which one you were."

She seemed almost surprised. "Oh? Why, my goodness—I thought you had us all figured out. You haven't made a mistake all day."

"I wouldn't know it if I had. Switch horses on me, and who knows if I'd figure you out?"

She said simply, "We haven't done anything like that, Kel. We've made no effort to confuse you."

"You dress alike, you look almost exactly alike, you talk alike . . ."

Again she seemed surprised. "But we don't do any of that to confuse you. These clothes are all we have right now. And the way we look and talk . . . well, that's just the way things are."

"Yeah, I know. But it bothers me a little. I mean, what if some poor fool fell in love with one of you. How would he ever know for sure he wasn't saying something meant only for the one to the other?"

For a very long moment she only looked at me. At last she said, "If anyone ever claims to have fallen in love with me, I would *expect* him to be able to tell me from my sister. I would *expect* him to know."

"But what if he couldn't be sure? What if he didn't always know?"

"I'm not sure," she said. "I just think he should know. He should know me well enough not to think me someone else, even my twin sister."

I thought about it. "Sometimes I think I can tell. You are two different people, of course. You have different personalities, different little ways about you. But there are other times . . . well, times when I just can't be sure."

She gave me a very intent look. "Maybe you don't know us well enough. Someone in love would know the person he loves better, don't you think?"

"But you said there was a way someone could be sure," I persisted. "A way all doubt could be removed."

She looked at me archly. "I believe I also told you it wouldn't do the least bit of good for you to know."

"Well, I guess I can accept that, all right. But you sure make my curiosity burn when you say it."

"Oh, is that so?" She straightened and turned somewhat back toward camp. "Well, I'm sorry. I guess your curiosity will just have to burn, because I'm not going to tell you."

I let silence speak my disappointment for me.

She said, "I'm tired. I think I'll go on to bed. Good night, Kel."

I watched her walk away and said, "Even if I fall in love with you, you won't tell me even then?"

I thought she broke stride just barely, and for a brief second, thought she might turn back. But she did not, which I decided was just as well. It left me to try to explain to myself why I had said such a damn-fool thing to a girl I hardly knew at all.

Morning dawned cold and clear again. Our fire had died out overnight, and I found it truly difficult to make myself leave my bedroll. I did so only upon realizing that one of the girls was already up. Quick little footfalls coming back from someplace caused me to roll over and look around. I sat up and found her suddenly crouched at my side.

She all but whispered as she spoke. "Did you mean what I think you were saying last night?"

I gawked at her, wondering if I'd heard right. Her expression was perfectly serious.

"Well?"

"I dunno," I finally blurted. "What . . . did you think I was saying?"

"You know very well what."

"I'm not sure what I meant. Something, I know . . ."

Those gray eyes bored into mine. Not looking very satisfied, she rose abruptly, and I knew the subject had been dismissed. "Should I build another fire?"

I threw back my covers. "How much bacon do we have left?"

"Maybe enough for one more meal."

I said, "It's up to you. If you want to eat, better build a fire. I'll go saddle the horses so they'll be ready to go when we need them."

I gave her the rest of my matches and went to get the first horse. The saddling of all three took about twenty minutes, during which time I did some thinking. A man doesn't have to know a girl well to at least *think* he's in love with her. But here I was, not even sure I knew the girl when I saw her. At least, not when she stood alongside her twin sister.

She had said someone who loved her would know. I didn't know if I loved anyone or not, but I did know if it could be either of these two girls, it was Etta. I just knew that. I just wasn't sure how to tell them apart, was all.

We ate bacon by taking turns plucking pieces from the skillet with my knife and talked about what to do next.

My view was already well-known. I wanted to go back to the dead horse and start there. The girls seemed unsure, but had little better to suggest.

"What possibly can we find there, Kel?" one of them asked. "A long-dead horse, our father's saddle . . . ?"

"Maybe something" was all I could say. "Something more than we've got any way else."

"I wonder where the Rutherfords are," she said. "That's another problem, you know."

I said, "It's also a reason we should make up our minds and get out of here. The longer we wait the more likely we are to find out where they are without really wanting to."

They agreed to break camp and go back in search of their father's dead horse.

We doused the fire, packed our small amount of supplies, and rolled up our bedrolls. We rode out, aiming for the head of the canyon and high ground. It turned out not to be easy.

The canyon took a sharp bend to the right, and its sides grew quite steep. We spent a good hour picking our way to the top, then found ourselves in thick timber, completely unsure which way to go to get back to where we were yesterday.

We decided to follow the ridge toward higher ground yet. After about half a mile we came upon a trail with horse tracks all over it. Horse and mule tracks. It seemed all three Rutherfords were astride mules.

I looked at the girls. "I think we spent all day yesterday and two hours this morning making nothing more than a big circle. These are day-old tracks: ours and theirs, I'll bet you."

They only looked at me.

I went on: "See that hill up there? That's where we stopped to rest and look around. All we have to do is follow our own tracks and we'll be where we want to go."

We made our way atop the hill over what was a familiar trail. Just as the day before, we stopped to rest our horses and view our surroundings. We dismounted and were stretching our legs when Etta called out, "Kel, look over there! Isn't that smoke?"

I followed her gesture. A thin spiral of gray smoke rose from beyond a ridge perhaps two miles away.

"Is it a campfire?"

"I'd bet on it," I said.

"The Rutherfords?"

I shrugged. "Could be."

"If it is," Ella said from nearby, "then who is that over there?"

A second curl of smoke lifted high above East Red Canyon a good mile to the east of the other smoke and over two miles from us. At first I had no idea what to make of either one; then I remembered something. I don't know why, but it had completely slipped my mind until then.

I said, "I never got a chance to say anything when it happened. It was day before yesterday when we were still with the Rutherfords. I thought I saw a couple of riders on a hillside some distance back of us. I didn't want to say anything your Cousin Henry would overhear, and I just completely forgot about it since. It was almost like someone was on our trail."

"But who?" Etta asked. "Who on earth could that be?"

"I have no idea. Could be only a coincidence they were there at all. I can't even swear I saw right."

"So, what does it mean now?" Ella asked.

"Who knows? Maybe nothing. One of those smokes is probably the Rutherfords. The other could be anybody. No telling which is which. Good thing about it is, neither one of them is very close. I'd say we go on about our business and let anybody that's after us worry about where we went."

We left the hill in the direction of the canyon where we had found Pete Ware's dead horse.

CHAPTER 16

WE rode single file. I got to worrying about those smokes. I said, "If one of those was the Rutherfords' campfire, why was it still burning two hours after we ourselves were already on the go? Wouldn't they be up and on our trail just as early as possible?"

Etta answered, "I wondered that, too."

Ella said, "Maybe they were just getting some extra rest. Maybe they weren't really that worried about catching us."

"How do you figure that?"

"Well, if they were following our tracks yesterday, don't you suppose they ran across Dad's horse in the process? I mean, wouldn't they finally figure just as we have that, there's the place to start from, no matter what we're doing?"

I said, "I'm not sure they found the horse. Whoever we saw on the point of that ridge probably never was in the canyon where we found it. Otherwise, I doubt he'd have been on the ridge."

The girls were both silent for a few moments. Finally Etta asked, "You think they lost our trail somewhere? That they stumbled onto us only by accident later on?"

"Seems possible. Good chance they split up to look. That could explain why we saw only the one rider, why he turned to go back rather than come straight after us."

"Which puts us back to wondering why they weren't up and about two hours ago, right?" Etta asked.

"It sure leaves *me* wondering that," I said.

"And what about the other smoke? Are you wondering about that, too?"

"Yeah, I am. But I have no idea what to make of it. Could be anybody."

"And which one do you think was the Rutherfords', if either was?"

Now there was a thought: What if neither campfire belonged to Cousin Henry and his crew?

We came to a place where yesterday we had left the trail to look off into one of the canyons. Three sets of mule tracks covered our own. Where we had turned around, a good deal of milling had taken place, especially by the mule riders. It became clear that the Rutherfords had not followed us back to the main trail, but had gone off a different way.

"Why did they do that?" Ella asked.

I had dismounted to look around. "I think they messed the trail up so much with their own tracks they couldn't tell where we went."

"Which would explain why they might never have found the canyon with Dad's dead horse in it," Etta concluded.

About ten-thirty we neared the spot where we had jumped two deer yesterday. There were plenty of fresh game tracks made since then, going and coming.

"You know," I said, "we followed those deer down there figuring there had to be water. All we found was a pitiful little seep. Now I figure there's too much good water in these mountains just now for those deer to be traipsing back and forth to drink from a muddy trickle."

"I guess we forgot about the deer tracks when we found the horse, didn't we?" Ella commented. "Maybe that's what we should have done—concentrated on the deer trail."

"Exactly," I said.

We were at the base of a hill, the top of which seemed to be reasonably free of trees. I was still bothered by those campfire smokes. It seemed a good opportunity to get someplace I could look back at them. I decided to take the time to make my way to the top for a look-see. The girls declined to follow along, both claiming a certain need for privacy dictated by Mother Nature and no real desire to make the climb anyway.

"Just don't be gawking back down this way while you're up

there," one of them said as I started off.

It took maybe ten minutes for me to make my way above the trees. I pulled up on a relatively flat area, just short of the hilltop, and dismounted. My view was little restricted to the north and east. I tried to relocate the positions of the campfire smokes and wound up wishing I had binoculars. I saw no sign of smoke anywhere.

I got to looking around to see what else I might spot. Tree cover blocked my view in many places, especially close in, but a high-flying bird couldn't have got a better look of much of the area. After a few minutes, during which I detected nothing untoward, I decided to mount up and go back down the hill.

The girls sat waiting for me beneath a split-topped pine, their horses picking at sparse grass close by.

"Spot anything?" one of them asked.

"Not much," I replied. "The smokes are gone, but I suppose that's to be expected by now."

They exchanged glances, which I thought looked somewhat conspiratorial. I was almost sure of this seconds later when they settled perfectly identical gazes on me and those gazes were simply a bit too innocent to be believed.

"Okay," I said guardedly. "What is it?"

The one on the left said, "We've decided to see if you can tell us apart."

I just stared at her.

"Well, can you?"

I stared some more. "Look, I don't know what you're up to, but is this really the time—?"

The one on my right said, "Why not? It won't take a minute. Come on. You've known us for several days now. Which one am I?"

I had a fifty-fifty chance and still hesitated. I didn't know; had no idea. It was strictly a guess.

I told the one who had spoken last, "Ella. I think you must be Ella."

They looked at each other and shook their heads in apparent disappointment. The one I'd called Ella got to her feet. "Come on," she told her sister. "I told you he couldn't tell."

"Now, look here . . . " I started to protest.

She didn't let me finish. "You were guessing; I know you were. Admit it. Even if you'd been right, it would have been by accident."

The other one got to her feet. "Are we ready to go?"

I stood silently and watched as they headed for their horses. Sure enough, the one I'd called Ella picked up the reins of Etta's gray. I shook my head in resignation and turned toward my roan.

I said, "I won't rest until I'm told how to tell you two apart for sure."

We followed our tracks of the day before toward the canyon, soon coming to the fork in the trail that had taken us to the dead horse. We paused long enough to notice that deer tracks were just as profuse on the right fork as the left.

I said, "You know, it could be these deer are feeding in that canyon and watering somewhere else. We may have fooled ourselves into thinking their going there meant the probability of a good spring."

"Now you tell us," Etta said.

"What about Dad's horse?" her sister asked.

"I'm just thinking if we don't find anything there, we might come back and try this right fork. Who knows where we'll find something."

We started down the left fork. I led the way, the girls following along single file. I don't think we had gone a hundred yards when I thought I heard something in the trees below us that I could swear sounded like voices. I pulled up abruptly.

"What is it?" Etta asked from right behind me.

"Shhh! Listen!"

For a moment there was nothing. Then I heard them

again. Someone calling to someone else. I couldn't understand what was said, but it sounded like someone calling a name.

"Did you hear it?" I asked in a low voice.

I looked back and was greeted with a pair of concerned nods. Ella asked, "Can you see anyone?"

"No, but I don't think they're very far away. Somewhere in those trees down there."

We waited nearly a minute longer. Nothing.

Etta asked. "Should we just be sitting here? Shouldn't we get out of sight or something?"

She was right about that. We were fully in the open, having gone about halfway across a small clearing when we heard the voices. I was just in the process of looking around for something to get behind when the first shot rang out. It ricocheted off a rock not ten feet away.

The shot had come from the trees dead ahead. A second followed even before we could turn our horses in retreat.

"Back up the trail!" I yelled. "Lead the way, Ella!"

She did, giving the heel to her sorrel without hesitation. Etta and I followed close behind. A third shot echoed behind us as we reentered thick tree cover.

When she reached the fork in the trail, Ella pulled up. Etta and I had no choice but to follow suit.

"Which way?" she asked.

I pointed to the fork we had only minutes before debated taking. I had no idea where it went, but I also didn't have much time to decide. From back down the trail came shouts, hoofbeats, and the sounds of someone crashing through brush.

Once again Ella led the way. The trail skirted around the right side of the nearest hill, then appeared to lead straight up a long ridge. I yelled ahead for the girls to rein in.

Our horses were already lathered and breathing hard. I looked back as I spoke. "I don't know if we can lose them this way or not. We leave a pretty easy trail to follow."

Ella asked, "Do you think they are the Rutherfords?"

"I'd bet on it."

"But why did they shoot at us?"

"I think they were shooting at me. I won't say I know why, except maybe they've finally decided they'd be better off without me around and have determined to do something more permanent than busting me over the head. That's why I'm thinking maybe we better split up."

For some reason Ella seemed the more concerned of the two. "But, Kel, what if we can't find one another again? What do we do?"

"You girls get out of these mountains as fast as you can, is what. Get somewhere you can get help. Anywhere. The first ranch you come to, Rosedale and the miners, Socorro—it doesn't matter which."

"And you? What about you?"

"Don't worry about me. If I can decoy the Rutherfords away from you, I'll do it. No matter what, I'll get away. Just worry about yourselves."

She looked unsure, not liking it at all. Etta, strangely, never said a word. I said, "Come on. We don't have time to dawdle or argue. Follow me. I'll show you where to leave the trail."

I didn't know exactly where that was going to be; I just figured I'd know a good place when I saw one. It wasn't that easy. A high peak rose to our left, its base a mile or more away. To our right was a yawning canyon, which drained generally northwest. I was pretty sure it was one I'd heard called Water Canyon, although I had never seen it from this vantage point before and could not be sure.

We came to another low hill with a rocky footslope. I pulled up once more. The trail went right, across rocks and gravel. To the left was no trail, a steep slope covered with trees. Behind us, in the trees, I heard someone yell. I didn't think they could see us but knew they would not be far from it if we hesitated long.

"Here is as good a place as any," I said. "You girls go left. Stay on the rocky slope as long as you can. I'll stay with the trail. Hopefully they will, too."

"But, Kel . . . " It was Ella again.

I said, "Don't argue. We don't have time. Just go. I'll find you again if I can. If not, just get away; get help to look for your father. We'll meet back up sometime. If worse comes to worse, you know where I live."

There was a crashing in the trees behind us, another yell. Someone said "This way! Their tracks go this way!"

"Now!" I said. "Go now!"

I watched for only a moment as they took to the slope and went quickly out of sight. Then I whirled my roan around and spurred for all I was worth on down the rocky trail.

The trail skirted the hill, then curled downslope toward Water Canyon. It was not an easy descent, and I was glad my roan was surefooted. Only out of desperation would I have taken such a trail.

Two or three times I stopped to watch and listen for signs of pursuit. Once I heard them yelling at one another again but could not see them. I was pretty certain they had at least started coming my way. All I could do was hope they hadn't discovered yet that they were following only one rider and not three.

It took a full half hour for me to negotiate my way to the bottom. The canyon was narrow at this point but promised to widen out as I went. I reined to a stop beneath a stand of towering fir, needing badly to let my horse regain his wind and hoping to catch sight of anyone coming down the slope behind me. The trees and brush were thick enough that I couldn't see much of the way I'd come, and I heard nothing.

I waited several minutes, and was about to give up, when suddenly I saw a rider top out on the point of a little ridge about halfway down. He was astride a mule. Seconds later, two more riders appeared, also on mules. I didn't think they could see me, for I was in the shade of those tall trees and pretty well-hidden as long as I didn't move. Nevertheless, they seemed to be looking my way. After a moment they retook the trail and disappeared in the trees and brush.

I calculated I had gained some time on them but did not have so much to spare I could tarry longer. Those mules would be even more surefooted than my horse and, if anything, might have the better stamina. Too, they hadn't been ridden for four days straight now. I had to make steady time but would also have to save my horse wherever I could. My best hope lay in the fact that someone following a trail is forced to stop more often than whoever they are trailing, lest the tracks be lost.

I made my way on down the canyon, following a good trail. As I went, I tried to recall the only time I had ever been in Water Canyon. I was pretty sure it had been two years ago when I had accompanied Monte and Ike on a bear hunt. We had come up West Red Canyon following three spotted hounds hot on a grizzly's trail. We had entered Water Canyon at its mouth and had lost the bear's trail about half a mile up its length. We had turned at that point and gone back.

That had been in the fall. A good stream of water had coursed its way down the canyon then.

I made little effort to hide my tracks, thinking that for now at least I wanted my pursuers to keep coming. The more time I could give the girls to get away the better. By the same token, I didn't want to make it too easy for the Rutherfords. I alternated between riding down a rocky creek bottom and staying on good ground. Presently I came to an area where there was water, mostly arising from seeps, and I rode in that.

After a while, I stopped to rest my horse again. I also needed to decide where I might go after leaving Water Canyon. Most likely, by then, I would become very serious about trying to lose my pursuers.

By the sun I calculated it was past noon, almost one

o'clock. I still had a good deal of daylight left to do whatever I was going to do.

West Red Canyon offered several possibilities. The two most obvious were to follow it up or down its length. If I went down the canyon, I figured after eight or nine miles I would have left the mountains altogether. I would also be at a point at least fifteen miles south of my homestead. If I went upstream, a much shorter distance, I would soon achieve the head of the canyon. That would take me back to within a couple of miles of where the girls and I had started the day.

I guess it boiled down to the fact that the easiest and surest way for me to escape my pursuers would be to do just as I had ordered Etta and Ella to do: Get out of the mountains. If I went down West Red Canyon, I would eventually come to a ranch or one of several mining towns to the south where I could get help. I doubted the Rutherfords would follow me far; as soon as they discovered what I seemed to be doing, they would probably turn back. The only trouble with that was, by the time I got help, a day and a half could go by just getting back to where I had last seen the girls. By then, no telling where they would be or what might have happened to them. The last thing I wanted was to simply abandon Etta and Ella.

Presently I made up my mind. I might have to do some fancy circling around to get there, but I determined to make it back to where I had parted with the girls. I knew which way they had gone and could possibly pick up their trail. It just seemed I had to try to relocate them the quickest way I could.

First, however, I had to do a good job of losing the Rutherfords.

CHAPTER 17

SOME things prove easier said than done. It was in the neighborhood of five o'clock. I stood atop a high hill overlooking a deep canyon that was almost completely in shadow. My horse was tied to an oak bush behind me, its saddle girth loosened and its head hanging. The animal was almost done in. Far below me, three riders on mules stuck doggedly to my trail. They were a good hour behind me now but were coming up on what I was beginning to think was my last hope to throw them off my trail.

They certainly were stubborn; I had little idea why. During the course of the day, I had done a lot of thinking about how they had almost caught us that morning. One thing I'd decided: If one of those campfire smokes had been theirs, they must have let the fire burn long after they had left it in order to get to where they were when we ran into them. Probably they had hoped we would see it exactly the way we had—not a bad decoy to make us think they were one place when they actually were in another. I suspected our encounter with them had been more by accident than not, but I considered it almost certain they had found our tracks of the day before in the canyon and had been backtracking us when they saw us. Likely, too, they had found Pete Ware's dead horse in the process. Maybe they thought we had found the hidden spring and cave, or at least had some track on where it was. Certainly by now they knew they were only following one rider; possibly they figured it was me. But did they want me out of the way so badly that they kept on following me so doggedly? I could only conclude that they did.

Well, I had tried one last ploy in the bottom of that canyon they were in. There was a fork down there. I had started my horse up one fork on soft ground, then alternated once again between that and a rocky creek bottom. In and out I'd gone, at first making sure they could pick up the trail every fifteen or twenty paces. Finally I had stayed with the creek bottom for over a hundred yards, then turned back. I rode like this all the way back to the other fork. If they were very careful, they would find an occasional hoofprint in the sand that mixed with the rocks and realize what I had done. By then their own tracks would make things difficult. I wasn't optimistic that I would lose them altogether, but at the worst I counted on their taking a good deal of extra time to figure me out one more time.

I had used the second fork to find a way out of the canyon, a rocky trail that eventually led to where I now sat. Even if I gained no more than another half hour on them, dark should eliminate any chance of them catching up to me today. With a moon nearing full, I felt I could find my way back at night to where I had left Etta and Ella. I couldn't do much more than that, because I couldn't track by moonlight any better than the Rutherfords could. But at least I would be that much farther along come daybreak tomorrow.

My main problem now was my horse. He had very little left in him. I had done my best to save him, but even that could not prevent the inevitable. Another problem: The girls had taken what food we had with them and I had given my last matches to Etta that morning. It was a bad time of year to find berries or nuts.

Of course, I would just have to get along without the food or the matches. The horse was another problem. Already I had decided to lead him wherever I could and ride only when necessary. But how far could I get on a bottomed-out animal, no matter what I did?

I watched the canyon for about five minutes more. Sure

enough, my pursuers took the wrong fork, very carefully staying with my first tracks. They soon went out of sight around a bend, and I turned to my horse.

"Well, son," I told him. "Looks like we both walk for a while."

I had a feeling I was going to be awfully footsore and weary before the day was over. I just wished I knew what I was going to do after that.

The sun was almost down by the time I reached a point not far from where the girls and I had escaped from the Rutherfords two nights before. I was atop the crest overlooking the canyon where we had been camped. The trail we had taken south that morning had horse and mule tracks all over it, some of them much fresher than others.

I took the trail south. Having walked a couple of tough miles already, I decided to ride. My roan was a valiant animal and showed willingness to give me all he had left.

I got to thinking about those horses we had turned loose in the Rutherford's camp the night we got away. They had been taken from the cow camp and belonged to Monte and Ike's cow outfit. They would know the way home and probably take it, which meant I had precious little chance of coming across one of them.

Dusk grew heavy around me as I plodded along. I jumped a deer and wished I had a rifle; I would have figured a way to get a fire started if I'd had fresh meat. Even a fat squirrel or a cottontail would have been welcome.

Only the faintest daylight still clung to the sky as I crossed a small clearing and approached a thick stand of trees. I guess I wasn't very alert to my surroundings, my mind on something else entirely, when my horse suddenly stopped and threw up his head, ears forward. He snorted loudly. It was more life than he'd shown in hours, and my first thought was that some kind of wild animal had startled him. Then I heard a soft nicker coming from within the trees. My horse answered with a whinny, and I just sat there dumbfounded as a rider on a gray horse appeared, ghostlike, on the trail.

"Kel—is that you?"

I rode on up to her and dismounted. "Etta! Where on earth did you come from?"

"I'm . . . not Etta," she said, also dismounting. "I'm Ella."

I was startled anew. "What do you mean you're not Etta? What are you doing on Blue Boy if you're not her?"

"I've ridden him almost all day, Kel. I'm sorry about it, I really am. We did something we hardly ever do anymore. We tricked you, and after we left you we just never got time to change horses again."

I stared at her. "Tricked me? How? Why? My God, when . . . ?"

She looked around and seemed to spot what she was looking for in a huge log lying alongside the trail. "Let me sit down, please. I'm just so tired I could drop. I can't believe I found you."

I watched as she settled wearily on one end of the log. I tied the horses, then went to stand before her.

I said, "Now, tell me what in the world you are talking about. Where *is* Etta? And how, for chrissake, do I actually know *which* one you are?"

She sighed. "I am Ella. It was the place where we stopped this morning—where you crawled up that hill to have a looksee. Etta talked me into it while you were gone. She said switch horses; she wanted to see if you could tell her from me. . . ."

For a moment I was speechless. "But why? Why would you do a thing like that?"

"I don't know why exactly, Kel. It's not like Etta to suggest such an idea. I am the one who always wanted to do those things. She just said, 'Do it and don't you dare give me away.' So I did it."

I wagged my head in disbelief.

"I am truly sorry, Kel. Honest, I am."

I took a deep breath and knelt before her. "Okay, okay. Never mind that now. What are you doing here? Where is Etta?"

She looked very tired, distraught. "I don't know where she is, Kel. I've been looking for her all afternoon. I—I couldn't find her. Oh, Kel . . ."

Suddenly I realized she was almost in tears. I took her by the shoulders. "Listen, calm down. You've got to make sense. Tell me what happened. How could you possibly have gotten separated?"

She wiped at her eyes. "That hillside you sent us down—it was too steep. We had to work our way around it and try another way. We wound up on a kind of shelf overlooking a canyon, and we couldn't find a way down there either. Finally Etta told me to stay where I was and she would scout ahead. I didn't want to, but she insisted. She went out of sight and didn't come back. I waited and waited. Finally I tried following her but I got lost. Once I thought I heard her calling but was afraid to call back; I was afraid the Rutherfords might still be close enough to hear. I tried to go toward her voice, but I never heard her again, and was so completely disoriented that I climbed back up that steep slope hoping I could get to a high place where I could see Etta. I never could. Then I got lost in the trees trying to get back to that canyon where I last saw her. I—I hardly know how I wound up here. I just now came onto this trail. It's—it's a miracle I found you . . ."

I still held her by the shoulders, although a little less demandingly now. "Ella, did you see anyone else all day?"

She shook her head. "No one. Not even at a distance. Oh, Kel—we have to find Etta! Something must have happened to her. I just keep thinking about my father's horse having fallen with him in that canyon, thinking what if the same thing happened to my sister? Oh, God, Kel—I couldn't handle that, I just couldn't!"

I sat down beside her. "Look, I'm sure you just got lost from each other. Like you say, you're lucky you found me. Between us, I'm sure we can locate where Etta went."

She looked at me. "It's dark, Kel. How will we ever find her in the dark?"

"Well, of course, we can't do a lot tonight. We can get back to where I left the two of you this morning, though. With the moonlight we'll have, I'm sure I can do that. We only have one real fork in the trail to worry about and all we have to do is take the one on the right. Tomorrow we'll be very close to where we want to start looking. We'll find her, don't worry."

"But, Kel. She's out there alone . . ."

"She's a tough girl, Ella. You should know that better than anyone. She'll be all right. I'm sure she will." I only wished I could be as confident as I sounded.

For a moment no one said anything. Finally I asked, "What condition is Blue Boy in? My horse is shot."

"He's all right," she said. "He hasn't done much except wander around all afternoon."

I said, "Good. You can ride while I walk and lead the roan. Maybe if I have to watch where I'm stepping I won't get lost. God knows, there's been enough of that for one day."

I almost bit off more than I could chew. It took a good two and a half hours to reach the place where I had left the girls that morning. Even then we might have stopped short a ways. I wasn't entirely sure of the exact spot, and I did not want to go past it.

We had neither food (Etta had our meager supply in her bedroll) nor water. I suppose we were both too exhausted to worry about it. We unsaddled and staked our horses out to graze, then rolled out our bedrolls and passed out in them with fewer than ten words between us.

I awoke with the sun in my eyes and couldn't believe it. Exhaustion had taken its toll. Ella was still asleep a few yards away. I had to shake her hard to get her to stir. At first she didn't seem to know where she was. She sat upright with a start and looked at me almost as if she didn't know me. Her hair was mussed and her eyes swollen.

I couldn't help a smile. "Don't worry," I told her. "I'm a friend."

She relaxed. "I—I must really have been asleep."

"You were dead to this world, I'll say. So was I. It must be eight o'clock already."

She grimaced. "I feel awful, Kel. My stomach is so empty it hurts. And the inside of my mouth and throat feels swollen. I want water, but I'm afraid if I drank I'd be sick."

"I know how you feel," I said. "This is pretty rough business, not the sort of thing a girl ought to have to endure. Soon as we find Etta, we're getting the hell out of these mountains. I'll guarantee you that."

Ella rolled up the bedrolls while I saddled the horses. My roan looked somewhat rested but I doubted he would take much hard work. I was afraid I'd ruined him.

We mounted up and started out. It didn't take long to find where the girls and I had separated yesterday.

"What if we can't find her, Kel?" Ella asked. "What are we going to do?"

"That may not be a problem," I said. "Look down there."

From two canyons away floated a thin spiral of campfire smoke. It might not have been Etta's, but I was willing to bet that it was. It would have been like her to take a chance that friends would spot her fire and beat her enemies to her side. If it was her, I had every intention of proving her right in that assumption.

CHAPTER 18

I could see what Ella meant about the steep slope I had tried to send them down yesterday. My guess was not many mountain goats would have tried it. We skirted the hillside the same way Ella said she and her sister had done, then made our way down onto an open shelf overlooking the head of a canyon that lay between us and the one from which the campfire smoke had risen.

The slopes here remained steep. We worked our way around to a ridge between one canyon and the next. By this time we were having trouble staying oriented with the location of the smoke we had seen, for we rode among thick trees and our destination was out of sight most of the time. Finally we crawled halfway up a hillside where we could see over the trees. The view of the canyon we wanted was excellent, but now we could no longer spot the smoke.

"Do you suppose she doused the fire?" Ella asked.

"I wouldn't be surprised. If it was even her . . ."

"Well, we know about where it was, don't we? We can still get there . . . can't we?"

I nodded. "Sure. If we can just find a way into the canyon. Maybe if we go that way—seems less steep down there." I was looking at a place farther down the canyon; a ridge slope that appeared to flatten considerably in the direction we needed to go.

We made our way off the hillside, then down a winding ridge through stands of tall pine and oak brush. We lost all sight of our destination again. There wasn't much for us to do but guess, and that is what we did. After a while, we came out on the point of a ridge and finally got a decent view again.

"Down that way," I said. "See that clearing in the bottom of the canyon?"

"I see it. I thought we would be closer, though. That must be half a mile away."

"That's true," I said. "But it's also not far from where that smoke was coming. I'd just about swear to that."

We finally found a deer trail that seemed to be going in the right direction. It only had one fresh track on it, but we didn't care at the moment about that. Our concern was to get to Etta the soonest way possible.

We found the campfire. It had been covered over with dirt and had been cold for at least an hour. There were small boot tracks all around, and nearby was where Etta must have staked her horse, for the grass there was either eaten or mashed down, and there were tracks and dung piles aplenty.

The camp had been located beneath a pair of giant fir trees, next to a small spring that trickled water into a clear pool a dozen yards away. There was no sign of Etta anywhere.

"Oh, I was so afraid of this!" Ella moaned. "Where did she go?"

"She's probably off looking for you," I said. "We'll just have to pick up her trail and follow till we find her."

It wasn't difficult. The tracks of a single horse led on down the canyon. The ground here was soft and she had followed a deer trail. We went about a half mile and found our canyon merging with a larger one. We crossed a little wash and found where she had turned up the larger canyon on a trail that had more tracks on it yet; some were horse tracks about two days old, going down-canyon; others were mule tracks perhaps a day old going the other way.

Ella and I looked at each other. I asked, "Does this canyon look familiar to you?"

"I . . . don't know. I've been so many places in the past few days. Maybe it does. Why?"

"I think these older tracks are ours. The others have to be the Rutherfords, made possibly yesterday. I think this is the canyon where we found your father's dead horse."

Her eyes grew wide as she looked around. "You may be right. What does it mean?"

"I don't know if it means anything. Etta's are the freshest tracks here, so I would say we just keep following them."

"Do you think Etta realized where she was?"

I shrugged. "She may have. Who knows?"

We didn't have to go far to prove ourselves right about where we were. The canyon forked, and just up the right-hand fork we found the dead horse. We also found total confusion in the tracks around it. Etta must have dismounted and looked around. So had someone else. There were numerous fresh boot prints, most larger than the girl's. There were also the unmistakable unshod hoofprints of the mules. Only these were fresher than the day-old ones we had been seeing. Finally I realized that all seemed to head right back the way we had come.

I said, "These tracks could all have been made this morning. And look which way they go when they leave here. I guess I didn't pay much attention to the trail after we passed that last fork."

Ella only stared at me.

"I think Etta was here, and then so were the Rutherfords. They must have come in from above. Etta went back down-canyon and so did they—the way we just came. There's a good chance they were either following her or chasing her straight out."

"Oh, my God, Kel! What are we going to do?"

"Follow them," I said. "What else can we do?"

One reason I hadn't detected the fresh tracks as we came that last hundred or so yards up the trail is they hadn't used the trail. My lousy tracking ability was challenged to the hilt just to follow something simple. The best I could tell as we backtracked, Etta had taken off at a gallop down a little wash, crossed to the other side, then turned up the other fork of the canyon. Mule tracks churned the ground all too frequently on top of hers, and they too had gone up the other fork.

We went at a trot, thinking to make what time we could, yet not to avoid caution completely. The little canyon twisted and turned. My roan stumbled more than once, and I knew his fatigue from yesterday was already catching up to him. Suddenly there was water in the creek bed. We rounded a bend and there was more. And once again, there was a good deal of confusion in the tracks.

I pulled up and dismounted quickly. So had our quarry. Animals and people had milled all about.

"Kel, look!" It was Ella. She pointed excitedly to a place across the creek bed, to a portion of the canyon wall that appeared to be solid rock, a bluff covered with grapevines and with water seeping at its base. Down low was a place where the grapevines had been pulled back. "Oh, Kel, just look!"

I handed her my reins and strode toward it, sloshing across the tiny stream, disregarding the water that got in my boots. I knelt down in front of the mass of vines. Someone had clawed wildly at them, pulling and yanking until a hole had been uncovered in the rock behind them.

I looked inside. It wasn't much of a cave, only a little water-worn nook that had probably taken centuries to carve out. I doubted if it was over three feet across or two feet high at its opening and suspected it was no deeper than it was wide. It was also the kind of place that would make a good snake den. I hesitated to test that possibility, despite the fact that someone else probably had just been there doing the same thing.

It was dark and I couldn't see well. Very tentatively, I reached inside and felt around. I found moist dirt, rocks, nothing else. I felt some more. Nothing. If anything had been there, it was gone now. I rose and looked around, and thus saw something I had almost missed altogether. Off to one side lay a pair of canvas bags, stiffened by time and full of holes probably chewed in them by rodents. I picked them up. Both were empty. I conjectured they had come from the cave and had been tossed aside as useless.

Bags in hand, I returned to where Ella held the horses. "This is all I found."

"Is it the cave, the hidden spring, Kel? Is it?"

"Somebody sure thought so," I said as I took my reins. "And if there was anything in there besides these old bags, they've already got it out. The question now is: Where did they go? And where's Etta?"

We looked around at the tracks for over five minutes. The only conclusion we could come to was that the entire lot of them had finally continued on up the canyon. We could not tell if Etta was with them or had preceded them, only that they had all gone the same way.

We slaked our now considerable thirst at the spring and watered our horses, then resumed following the tracks up the trail. I didn't say so to Ella, but I was almost certain her sister had been taken captive by the Rutherfords once more.

They had left the canyon on a winding deer trail that led back toward the mountain crest. My roan was played out, and it was all he could do to make it to the top with me leading him halfway. Surprisingly, the tracks at the top led on up the ridge to the south.

"Now why would they be going that way?" I wondered aloud.

Ella heard, but did not offer a suggestion. I think she knew that they must have Etta. The poor girl was so exhausted she hardly had the energy to even talk anymore. I knew how she felt. How I had made it to the top of the ridge leading that horse I still don't know. One thing I did know: We had to stop and rest; there just were no two ways about that.

We drew up in a shady little place surrounded by tall trees.

This happened more by accident than anything else. Ella dismounted and plopped down on the ground in total exhaustion. I pulled the saddles from both horses and staked them nearby. My roan just stood there with his head down. I went over and sat down beside Ella.

"I don't know what to do next," I told her. "We're practically on foot, we have no food or weapons, and I reckon we're pretty close to helpless."

Ella's voice was dry and cracked. "You think they have my sister, don't you? You don't think she got away from them?"

"I have no way of knowing for sure," I said.

She didn't reply to this. I think she was just too tired. She rolled over on her side, and I swear she must have fallen asleep while I watched. After a bit, I decided I might as well do the same. I pulled my saddle around for a headrest and probably lasted about as long as Ella had after that.

A horse nickered softly from nearby, then whinnied. An answering whinny came from farther away. I sat up blinking, a late afternoon sun in my eyes. I wasn't thinking very clearly or very fast, but I did know that someone was coming. In my foggy mind, it had to be the Rutherfords.

I reached over and shook Ella by the shoulder. She groaned. I shook her again. She rolled onto her back.

"Wake up," I said. "Hurry. Someone's coming."

I was on my feet and carrying my saddle toward the horses when they appeared, coming out of the trees. Four riders. It was too late, no chance we could get away.

"Kel! By God, it's Kel! Kel and the girl!"

I stared in disbelief as my friends Monte and Ike and two others came riding up and dismounted before us.

One of them had to be helped from his horse. He rode with one leg sticking almost straight out, in a crude but effective-looking splint. Of the four, he was the only one I had never seen before. Ella, on the other hand, knew him instantly.

"Dad! Oh, my God, Kel—it's my father!"

CHAPTER 19

MANY times I'd observed men who were in no shape to do so ride horses, but I could not recall seeing one with a broken leg like that making the attempt. Pete Ware—for that is certainly who he was—had sure been doing it, and if anybody ever looked like he should be riding a bed instead of a horse, he did.

For several minutes, all was total confusion: Ella jumping to her feet and running to embrace her father, crying and jabbering incoherently all the while; Monte and Ike standing off to one side, beaming at what I suppose they figured was some great accomplishment on their part; the fourth rider in the group hovering nearby, virtually ignored; and me, simply standing there agape, completely unable to accept any of it as real.

Pete Ware was of medium build and about my height, but he did not look well. His face, behind a month's growth of beard, appeared drawn and haggard, and his eyes were sunken. His daughters had never described him to me, but in listening to their talk about him I had come to picture him as healthy and robust.

The foursome had with them a packhorse and two riderless mounts that looked very familiar to me. I would swear this latter pair were among the three we had turned loose that night when we escaped the Rutherfords' camp. The fourth man I knew as the sheriff of Socorro County, a man named Ed Pickering. I had met him in Magdalena only a few months before. Presently it occurred to me to suggest we all sit down and do as quick a job as we could of swapping pertinent stories about what had been going on. After all, I pointed out, Mr. Ware had two daughters involved in this and one of them was most likely still in the hands of Cousin Henry Rutherford and his two sons, with no telling what in store for her.

Pete Ware was helped over to a place where he could sit down with reasonable comfort, and the rest of us gathered around. Ella clung to her father as if never to let him go again.

Monte spoke for his group. "Damm it, Kel, you don't know how worried we was about you. Sure as hell, it's gonna be hard to keep our side of the story short!"

"Try," I said. "Just give it your best."

"Well, all right, here goes," he said. "It has to start with the last time you saw us and we saw you, that late afternoon when those jaspers ambushed us and we got separated. Me and Ike hunted for you all the next day without any luck. We just could not pick up your trail. Finally we decided the way things was, it was time to go for help. We went back to the cow camp and found everybody but the cook out on the roundup. It was then we decided wasn't nothin' for it but to go to find Ed Pickering. Too much had happened that should involve the law. As luck would have it, we run into Ed at Magdalena, and he agreed to help us run down this crew of mule and horse thieves that had shot at us in the San Mateos. That and to help find our good friend Kel, who we didn't know what had happened to."

He paused, and I said, "Go on."

"Well, the roundup crew was gone again from the camp, and we'd already lost better than two days, so we didn't have time to hunt up more help, and it was just the three of us. By the time we got back to where the ambush took place, all trails was cold. We looked all over and finally wound up goin' over to your place on the west side. We found signs of you havin' been there but little sure sign where you'd gone. We headed back into the mountains and wandered around another day. We thought we had a fresh trail picked up one time, comin' up the crest here, but then we lost it. Finally we went over to Rosedale to see if any of the miners there had seen anything unusual lately and they said they sure had. It was then we got introduced to this gent here, Mr. Pete Ware."

Ella and I were listening with rapt attention and did not interrupt. Monte went on: "Now, as you know, we didn't know a thing about this man's story and had no idea it connected up with you or our hunt for them mule thieves. But the minute we started to describe the mule thieves we was lookin' for, and as soon as we heard the tale them miners had to tell about Pete Ware—well, we knew we all had somethin' more in common than just the love for a good story."

It was Ike who finally butted in. "That's for damn sure, Monte. And you're sure as hell not keepin' yours short!"

Monte glared at him. "You think you can do better?"

Ike didn't need any more of an opening that than. "Let me tell you right here and now, it took some doin' to get it all straight. A couple of them miners had found Pete Ware over in East Red Canyon over three weeks ago, draggin' himself on his belly through mud and snow, half-starved, plumb out of his head with fever, and one leg broke bad just below the knee. He couldn't tell 'em nothin' that made sense about where he'd been or what had happened to him, not even who he was. So they set his leg, rigged up a travois to carry him on, and took him back to Rosedale. There he's been ever since, rantin' and ravin' about needin' to get home but unable to tell anybody anything that would help 'em figure out where that was. Seems he couldn't even remember his own name to tell 'em that. They didn't know what to do with him but try to feed him and get him well. Seems they figured on eventually sendin' for Ed Pickering to come and do something, but they put that off till they could make sure the poor fellow was even goin' to live."

"So, how did you finally learn Pete Ware's story?" I asked. I looked at the subject of the discussion. "I assume you were able to tell them something yourself by then."

There was a wry little glimmer in the man's eyes as he was spoken to directly. "I guess the condition I was in when they found me is called shock. I was also half-burned-up with fever. I remember almost nothing for a period of what must have been a full two weeks. When I finally did start to come out of it, the last thing I recalled was a bad snowstorm and my horse falling with me. I remember knowing my leg was broken and stripping my bedroll and rifle from my saddle. After that, nothing. By the time these fellows arrived in the mining camp, though, I had come out of it fairly well. Maybe you know my story well enough by now, Mr. O'Day, to understand why I still hadn't told anyone why I came to these mountains. I knew I had to get back to Colorado, but I also knew I was in no shape for the trip yet under any circumstances. I guess you could say I spent about one week of my stay in Rosedale pretending a loss of memory. Before that, in all my life I've never been so purely out of my head."

"And your story, the reason you were in these mountains," I said. "Did you tell it to these men here?"

He nodded. "They told about these three fellows who had stolen some mules and some horses and had ransacked a cow camp. From the description I understand you gave of them and a girl who was with them, I knew we were talking about the Rutherfords and at least one of my daughters. It never once occurred to me that Henry would bring my girls here. I knew I couldn't trade on their safety just to protect myself. I went ahead and told these men, including the sheriff, my whole story."

I looked at Ed Pickering, who I had never heard was anything but a good and fair man. He said, "I don't know anything about any mine payroll robbery that happened in another man's county fifteen years ago. But I don't tolerate horse thieves—mule thieves, either, I reckon—in my jurisdiction. If you can help us run down these Rutherfords and get this man's daughter back, then that's all I'm interested in, Kel."

I smiled, looked first at the position of the sun, then toward the packhorse and the two riderless animals the recent arrivals had brought with them.

I said, "And all I ask, folks, is some food, a gun, a fresh horse, and a chance to make use of about two more hours of good daylight. Ike, maybe you could stay here with Mr. Ware and Ella. I figure Monte, Ed, and I can go after the Rutherfords." I turned to Pete Ware. "Ella can tell you what we've been through. If a man ever had reason to be proud of his daughters, you'll be proud of yours, let me tell you."

We sat our horses atop the point of a low ridge overlooking Water Canyon, the setting sun at an angle to our left. Below and down-canyon from us, less than a mile away, four riders had dismounted and seemed to be unsaddling their animals. We were sure they were the Rutherfords and Etta about to make camp. We had followed their circuitous trail for over an hour and a half and had just now got them in sight.

"We found the hidden spring and the so-called cave," I was telling Monte and the sheriff. "So did they. If there was anything in there, they got it. All I found were two empty canvas bags half eaten by rats. I guess Pete Ware got awfully close before his horse went down with him. Could be he never knew how close he really was."

Monte wagged his head. "We must have missed you half a dozen times over the past two days. I'm positive one of those campfire smokes you saw was ours. We wasted half a day chasin' the other one down ourselves, only to find whoever had made it had gone off and left it to burn out on its own."

Ed Pickering said, "I never saw many tracks going every which way on so many trails. Every time we thought we'd picked up a promising one, we got distracted by another one."

"We found those two horses running loose two days ago,"

Monte said. "They wore my outfit's brand, and I figured they were two of those stolen by your mule thieves. The other one must have got lost or gone on home."

Ed Pickering looked thoughtful. "You know, Pete Ware told us that mine payroll was all in gold coin. That mine company paid their men that way. It would not have been a light load. Somehow I doubt those Rutherfords had the time to transfer something like that from those canvas bags, or the wherewithal to carry it."

"Could be," I said. "Could be it was already gone. Someone else could have found it anytime in the last fifteen years. Maybe that's why they've still got Etta. Could be they still think Ware pulled one on them, and if they ever find him, they'll have his daughter to hold over him for it."

Monte said, "You gotta figure it this way, too, Kel. If that girl's the spittin' image of her sister, I wouldn't trust those Rutherfords or anybody like 'em not to take her for another reason. Maybe they figure to take out on her what they couldn't get out of her father."

I had thought of that myself. I didn't need to be reminded. I didn't say anything.

"Well, Ed," Monte said after about a minute. "What's the plan?"

The sheriff shrugged. "Looks made to order to me. They're making camp. Be dark by the time we get down there, but that'll only be to our advantage. We've got a good moon, and if they build a fire, they'll be sitting ducks for us to surround."

Dark found us in the bottom of the canyon short of the Rutherfords' camp and unable to see their fire. We had seen it while coming down from that ridge earlier. But like so many of the places we all had been during the past few days, the slopes were steep and not quickly negotiated.

We rode in moon shadows sharply contrasting with brightly moonlit ground. Never in my life had I done anything quite like this. We were creeping up on a hopefully unsuspecting camp, intent on taking armed men any way we had to.

I carried weapons for the first time in days, Ike's Winchester .44-40 rife and .44 caliber handgun, tucked in my belt. Ed Pickering was in the lead, and I was glad about that. He was a good man who knew his job and was not about to take foolish chances. Monte Preston was more like me, a simple cowhand who was not accustomed to such duty. Nonetheless, he was a steady fellow who could be counted on in a pinch. Look what would have been my lot had it not been for the persistence of Monte and Ike.

A dancing flicker of flame suddenly revealed itself through the trees ahead. We pulled up.

Ed Pickering said, "I think we'd best leave the horses here. They'll only give us away if we take them any closer."

We tied our mounts carefully to nearby bushes and hung our spurs across our pommels.

"Check your weapons," the sheriff warned. "One in the barrel. No use going any other way."

"Just don't forget Etta," I said. "No shooting if she's in the way."

"I know," the sheriff said. "Don't worry."

We crept forward, the sheriff in the lead. In a matter of minutes we were within hearing distance of the camp. The four of them sat around it, Etta between the boys, Cousin Henry directly across from her.

The older Rutherford's voice carried well in the night. "The truth of the matter is, girl—somebody beat us to that stash. Those grapevines were pulled back and the bags empty when we got there. Either your friends or your pa did it. I don't figure to rest till I find out which. And you're ours till that time comes. It's as simple as that."

"I've told you and told you," Etta replied wearily. "It was like that when I found it, too. I don't know where my sister and Kel O'Day are, and my father would never have done that. You're wasting your time holding me."

"Come on, Pa," Billy Rutherford said. "Let's forget it. Let's just take the girl and leave these mountains." He looked lewdly at Etta. "Hell, I'd trade all of it for her, anyway. Just let me have her, Pa. For chrissake, be reasonable."

I felt my jaw muscles tense and almost didn't feel the sheriff's hand on my shoulder. He whispered, "You stay here; be ready. I'm going to get around them. Monte, you come with me."

I sat quietly gripping my rifle and waiting as my companions moved softly off into the shadows.

After a moment, Henry Rutherford rose and looked away from the fire. "Come on, Shank, let's go check the mules. Billy, you watch the girl, but hands off, you understand?"

They disappeared in the darkness outside the firelight. Once again I grew tense as Billy Rutherford turned toward Etta. He said something in a low voice.

Etta's reponse was anything but low-pitched. "Shut your filthy mouth, Billy Rutherford! You'll never be man enough to say something like that to me!"

I found myself crouched and ready to charge. It was all I could do to stay put. Seconds later, Cousin Henry and Shank returned. They were approaching the fire when all of a sudden a voice rang out:

"Hold it right there! Don't move! This is Ed Pickering, sheriff of Socorro County. You are under arrest!"

Henry Rutherford and his older son were no fools. They had no chance and they knew it. They froze in their tracks. Ed Pickering and Monte emerged from the camp's darkened fringe, rifles poised.

"Any weapons on you, put them slow and easy on the ground," the sheriff ordered.

Cousin Henry and Shank did as they were told, laying handguns at their feet and instinctively raising their hands. It almost seemed too easy.

And it was. Billy Rutherford saw to that. Almost quicker than the eye could blink, he had Etta, his left arm around her neck from behind and his six-gun in his free hand. He pulled her to her feet and started backing away from the sheriff and Monte, shielding himself with the girl as he went. For some reason he never said a word, he just kept backing away, pulling the girl with him.

He backed directly toward me. He kept coming, and I just kept standing my ground, waiting.

Finally, when he must have figured he was well behind the firelight, he stopped. He was still about ten feet from me. "Okay, sheriff, put your rifle down. Both of you."

"Don't be an idiot, boy," Ed Pickering said. "You want me to blow your pa all the way into Arizona? You harm that girl, and that's just what I'll do."

Clearly Billy didn't have what it took to call a bluff. He backed away some more. Even as he made his last step, I seemed to recall Shank once saying Billy was the one who had hit me over the head when they stole my mules and again when they recaptured Etta at the cow camp. I decided Shank probably hadn't been lying, and was not a bit sorry for what I was about to do as I raised the butt of my rifle and brought it crashing against his unsuspecting skull.

CHAPTER 20

WE arrived back on the mountain crest with three prisoners in tow at midmorning the next day. Ike, Ella, and Pete Ware had seen us coming and were waiting as we rode up. Ike had only recently returned from a spring in a nearby canyon where he had filled two canteens and had coffee boiling on the fire.

Henry Rutherford looked at Pete Ware and said, "Well, you won out again, Pete. What did you do with the money this time?"

Pete Ware only shook his head. "Don't know what you're talking about, Henry. I never made it to the stash. If you didn't get it, then I don't know who did. Someone else, sometime during the past fifteen years, must have got lucky. That's all I can say."

Sheriff Pickering dismounted and walked over to the fire. "That coffee smells awful good to me this morning. Reckon I could use some of that before heading out for Socorro with these fellows. Monte, you and Ike wanta help me take them in?"

"Sure, Ed," Monte said. "Beats roundup dust and burnin' hair any day."

Ike didn't have anything to say. Clearly Monte spoke for both of them.

I looked at the three Rutherfords. They sat their horses, hands tied to their saddle horns, looking pretty dismal. Billy looked the worst. He had a bandage around his head where my rifle butt had split the skin. For a while I thought I had killed him, it took so long to bring him to. I knew a lot about how it felt, but I still didn't feel sorry for him.

"What will happen to them, sheriff?" one of the girls asked.

"Well, they're gonna face some charges. Mule and horse theft, ransacking that cow camp, assault and battery, attempted murder. Don't worry, they won't get off easy in front of a Socorro County jury. No chance of that."

"And my father? Will he get in trouble when his story comes out?"

He smiled. "I can't guarantee I have total control over that, but I certainly haven't found any evidence of his wrongdoing. Besides, as I told you before, that was in another place a long time ago. I wouldn't worry about it, if I were you. Possibly, you will have to hang around for a while, just in case your testimony is needed, but your pa doesn't look up to a trip to Colorado yet anyway. Maybe Kel could put you folks up at his place for a few days till we know."

"I had already thought of that," I said. "I was going to offer soon as the time seemed right."

"That's very kind of you, young man," Pete Ware said.

"One other thing, Ed," I said. "What about my mules? Are you going to have to have them to get these follows to Socorro? May not seem like much to anybody else, but I got into this deal because of those mules and I still want them back."

The sheriff laughed. "You'll get them, Kel. I'll see to that personally. Hope you get as good a price on them over on the Blue River as you expected, too."

I shook my head at that. "I've been thinking about keeping them. They're good saddle animals, and I can use them. Especially since I lost one horse back at the cow camp and this roan here is likely ruined."

An hour later we watched the sheriff, Monte, and Ike ride away with the Rutherfords. I turned to the girls and their father. "We'll go a different way to get to my place, so no use riding even partway with them. Just tell me when you're ready to head out."

"We'll be ready when you are," one of the girls said.

I looked at her. "Etta?"

"Yes."

"I thought so. Will you come help me with your father's and Ella's horses?"

She gave me a strange little look, then glanced hurriedly at her father and sister. "Ella, Dad, you be getting ready. I'll only be a moment."

The two horses were staked beyond a small thicket of oak brush, just out of sight of the camp. We went to catch them and bring them back. When we were past the brush thicket, I stopped and turned to Etta. She seemed startled.

"How can I be sure?" I asked.

"W-what? I don't know what you mean . . ."

"You say you're Etta. How can I be sure?"

"Why, I just told you. Isn't that good enough?"

"Not anymore. You tricked me once. What's to keep you from doing it again?"

She blushed slightly. "Oh, that. Well, I . . . I wouldn't do that again. I mean . . . it was only to see if you . . . if you . . ."

"To see if I could tell you apart," I finished for her. "Yeah, I know. But I told you all along I couldn't always. And when you deliberately set out to fool me, well, it was nigh on impossible. No, you've got to tell me how it is I can be sure. You owe me that, Etta."

She blushed even more. "Kel! I *can't* do that. If you knew . . . you wouldn't even ask."

"But I don't know, and I am asking. You've got to tell me, that's all there is to it."

She was beginning to look almost desperate. "Please, Kel. Not here, not now. If-if you should later decide you really . . . well, care for me . . . perhaps I'll tell you then."

I had determined on a relentless course, and I was not about to give up now. "I've already decided that, Etta. I think you know that. And I was beginning to think I could tell you from your sister, till you pulled that low-down trick on me.

Now I won't give up till you tell me."

She looked around nervously. "But, Kel, what if Ella comes, my father . . . ?"

"Tell me now or I'll make you do it in front of them. Tell me, Etta."

Finally her shoulders sagged in resignation, those gray eyes dropping to my chest. "You don't know how awful this is for me, Kel. You don't know—"

"Tell me!"

She looked up and straightened, perhaps a bit defiantly. "Okay . . . I will. But you are going to be ashamed of yourself. Believe me, you will."

I just stood there, waiting.

"When I was a little girl," she started hesitantly, "I fell off the porch of our house in Colorado. I landed on some boards on my chest. Some of the boards were broken and had jagged ends. I . . . cut myself . . . here." Eyes lowered, she placed a hand on her left bosom. "It wasn't very serious, but it left a scar. . . ." She paused and raised her eyes bravely to meet mine. "So, you see, the one sure way to tell me from my sister is that scar. It is two inches long and very ugly. I have hated it forever."

I was taken aback more than I wanted to let on. I'd had no idea it was something like that. Still, something devilish in me wanted to get back at her for the poor trick she and Ella had played on me.

I said, "Show me."

Her eyes flew up to mine. "Oh, Kel! You don't mean you would make me do that! Why, I won't! I can't!"

"If that is the only way I can be sure which of you is which, then show me. I'm telling you something I don't ever want to tell anyone else; I aim to be sure I'm saying it to the right girl."

Her face was crimson, but her resolve melted almost instantly with my words. I guess she thought she saw something very unrelenting in my look. She dropped her eyes again and brought her fingers to the top button of her shirt.

She looked at me once, almost beseechingly, before dropping to the second button. The top two were undone and her fingers fluttering nervously at the third when I quickly clasped her hands together and stopped her. I could already see the deliciously white upper flesh of her breasts, but I could not let her go further.

"No, Etta . . . God, no. You don't have to. I know who you are. I can tell. You've proved all you need to."

She collapsed against my chest, and for a long moment I held her tightly. Then someone was calling: "Etta! Kel! Where are you with those horses?" It was Ella. "What are you doing over there?"

I released Etta just enough that I could look at her face. Tears glistened in those gray eyes, but they did not hide the happy smile that went with them.

A short while later we broke camp and helped Pete Ware—albeit precariously—onto his horse, which was a gentle sort especially selected for the duty. Ella kept giving Etta strange looks, but all she got in return was a beaming smile. We were ready to ride away, but Pete Ware seemed to want to linger. He only sat there, the look in his eyes faraway, cast in the direction of the little canyon with the hidden spring.

"Dad," Etta said. "What's the matter?"

"What's that? Oh, well, I was just thinking about all the hell that foolish thing I did fifteen years ago has caused, about how I pray it never comes back to haunt any of us again."

Etta's eyes narrowed with suspicion. "Dad—is there something you're not telling us?"

He turned back to us, a strange expression on his face, one I don't think I could ever describe.

Etta's eyes narrowed even further. "Dad, when I found that spring and the cave yesterday, those grapevines were already partly pulled back. The Rutherfords cleared them away even more, but what I saw first didn't look like something done only a day or so ago. More like weeks."

He met her gaze and presently smiled. It was almost a

sheepish smile. He glanced at me. "Can this young man be trusted?"

"Dad! How can you ask that? Why, look what he has done for us!"

He looked thoughtful. "All right. But it must remain a secret among the four of us. Is that agreed?

"You see, I lied a little bit. I was hardly injured at all when my horse fell with me that day in the snowstorm. A few scratches is all. I took my rifle and bedroll and went on to the place I'd made my stash. It was only a short distance, as you know. It was later, as I made my way down the canyon on foot, that I fell from a boulder and broke my leg and wound up dragging myself in shock through the snow and lost all memory of the next couple of weeks."

"And the money, then? Was it already gone when you got to the spring and the little cave?"

He smiled as he said, "No, it was there, every dollar of it, I'm sure. But that's the end of it. I knew there was nothing Henry Rutherford could really do if I told him someone had already got it. I hid it again, and this time I'll never tell a soul where. Not even you three. I hid it so no one will ever find it or know it's there. No one, not ever again."

If you have enjoyed this book and would like to receive details of other Walker Western titles,
please write to:

Western Editor
Walker and Company
720 Fifth Avenue
New York, New York 10019